KENTUCKY (SPECIAL FORCES: OPERATION ALPHA)

NEMESIS INC. BRAVO TEAM

BOOK TWO

BELLA STONE

Dear Readers,

Welcome to the Special Forces: Operation Alpha Fan-Fiction world!

If you are new to this amazing world, in a nutshell the author wrote a story using one or more of my characters in it. Sometimes that character has a major role in the story, and other times they are only mentioned briefly. This is perfectly legal and allowable because they are going through Aces Press to publish the story.

This book is entirely the work of the author who wrote it. While I might have assisted with brainstorming and other ideas about which of my characters to use, I didn't have any part in the process or writing or editing the story.

I'm proud and excited that so many authors loved my characters enough that they wanted to write them into their own story. Thank you for supporting them, and me!

READ ON!

Xoxo

Susan Stoker

ACKNOWLEDGMENTS

Thank you to my Sailor for always having my back. You have owned my heart for almost three decades, and you will always be my hero—even when you make me insane, and I find pens and other crap from your pockets in the dryer. You and our amazing kiddos, Potterhead and Pottermonkey—you make this crazy life worth it.

Thank you, the family of my heart, who not only claimed me as theirs, (in public I might add…) who read this story as it was written, answering all my military questions, and helping ensure my information is as factual as possible. Any mistakes I have made are mine. Thank you for the middle of the night conversations and virtual smacks upside the head that were needed to keep me on track.

Thank you to my Operators. All y'all put up with my crazy, without a second thought. You laugh at my silly memes, and you love the stories and characters in my head as much as I do. I am forever grateful to have y'all in my life. #Lovelikeanoperator

I'd also like to take this opportunity to thank the god who discovered that Coffee is an amazing way keeping my eyelids propped open when the characters in my head are yelling out their stories at 3 AM… Without the aid of the coffee gods, these stories would never be written.

#Neverforgotten
For the 31 heroes of Extortion 17.

Brothers don't always have the same mother.
Until we meet again to feast in the halls of Valhalla.

Special Warfare Operator
Petty Officer 1st Class (SEAL/Enlisted Surface Warfare Specialist)
Jon T. Tumilson

A NOTE FROM THE AUTHOR

I have been a Susan Stoker fan since I first read Beyond Reality when it first came out. When Protecting Caroline hit my kindle, I became a huge fan, and I landed firmly on the Stalker Posse. It's been a dream and an honor to be allowed to borrow The SEALs of Protection Heroes and to write them into my world. Susan, thank so you very much for allowing me to play in your sandbox. Being allowed to borrow your characters is a dream come true. I can never thank you enough for the opportunity you so graciously gave me. I really hope I did Wolf, Caroline, and the rest of the SEALs of Protection family, the justice they deserve.

Some of the biggest thank yous has to go to Riley and Olivia, both of these ladies sprinted with me, cheered me on, and reminded me to practice what I preach and follow my dreams. Both of you are my tribe, there will never be a time that you call, and I won't drop everything and come running. Thank you both for sprinting through long nights and too many days to count. This story is what it is, because I have you two as my sprinting sisters. I adore you both.

Stalkers and Operators, magic happens when you trust your gut and follow your dreams.

#LoveLikeAnOperator.
XO
Bella

PROLOGUE

LAKE BLUFF, ILLINOIS

"Fuck my life. Kara—freaking—oke." Kentucky Smith scowled at the equipment being dragged onto the stage. "Hey, Ma?" There weren't any customers in the bar at this time of the afternoon, so yelling wouldn't earn him a scolding. Not that he minded those so much these days. Life had a way of kicking a SEAL in the balls, and he'd discovered even if he was a badass, there were some things only his mom's home cooking could fix. Until right this second, he'd thought coming home for the first time in way too long had been an awesome idea.

"Do you need seconds?" his mother called from the kitchen behind the bar. "I told you to take more. You didn't have enough food on that plate to feed a bird, never mind a growing boy."

"Sure." He wasn't going to argue with her that he was no longer a growing boy. With almost twelve years in the US Navy and most of it spent in Special Warfare under his belt, growing boy wasn't anything close to what he was anymore. She'd worried enough about him over the last few years. The least he could do was let her mother him a bit. The fact her cooking was still the best he'd ever tasted helped, too. "Are we doin' karaoke tonight?"

"Yes." She came through the swinging doors with a plate in her hand. "The latest class is graduating boot camp up at Great Lakes, and karaoke keeps them here most of the night. It's becoming one of our biggest nights of the year."

How could he complain when the freshly graduated seamen were keeping their family bar in the black? His momma would remind him putting up with noise and drunks for a couple of hours a night kept a roof over her head. He sighed and pushed his empty plate to one side, making room for the one she carried. "They'll be squalling like a bunch of sick crows by nine."

"True." His mom ran her hand over the top of his head. "But if they're squalling, they aren't fighting, and that's always a bonus."

"Yeah." He'd been planning on meeting up with some of his friends tonight. But he'd call them and invite them to the bar instead of going somewhere else. Just in case shit hit the fan, he wanted to be here. "Me and the boys will be here shooting pool for a while tonight."

"Tommy and Scott?"

"Yeah."

"I'll have goodies in the kitchen."

"Thanks, Ma." He hadn't needed her to tell him there would be homemade cookies and probably a cake waiting for them behind the bar. The boys had been his best friends since they'd moved here when he was in high school, and all of them spent a lot of time in this bar. Homework had been done at this table, and after-school snacks fed them all. His momma had recognized that Scott didn't have the best home life and had loved him just a little bit harder to make up for it.

She squeezed his shoulder. "Eat up. If the boys are

coming, I need to get busy as I'm going to need a millionaire's shortbread for Scott."

"He's still your favorite kid, huh?"

"Shh, you. You know I love all three of you." She plopped her hands on her hips. "I was gonna make muffins for you and Tommy, but I think I might have just about changed my mind."

"Careful, Ma, or I'll be the one up there," he jerked his thumb at the stage, "and running everyone out of here while I make them listen to my version of Celine Dion."

"Kevin!" his mother yelled at the man who'd stocked the bar for as long as Kentucky could remember. "Get the hose ready for tonight. If Ken so much as sniffs at that microphone, douse him with it."

"Yes, Ma'am." The retired Navy veteran grinned at them over the top of the bar. "I'll run down to the hardware store in a bit and get a fresh nozzle, just to be sure I can hit him at full power."

He sliced off some of the meat and forked it into his mouth. Damn, he'd missed this. "Y'all are mean."

"Look at you talkin' like the southerner you were born as. I love that you haven't lost your accent. You sound like your father."

He'd missed his mother's teasing and the comfort of being home in this place. Many might say a bar wasn't a place to raise a kid. He didn't agree. This was his comfort zone. He could sling beers with the best of them. The smells, the sounds, and the welcome feeling of home when he walked in the door soothed all the aching spots in his soul.

"Finish your food, son." Ma turned away toward the bar. "Go find your other two stooges and I'll get to baking."

He smiled after her retreating back and then scowled at the stage again. "Freaking karaoke. Hopefully, it won't be too bad."

* * *

YOU FUCKING JINXED IT. You should know better than to hope shit wouldn't be too bad.

"Jeez, he'd fit in better out back with the alley cats." Kentucky smacked Tommy's hand away from the biggest muffin and winced as the dude on the stage murdered his second song in the space of five minutes.

"Yeah." Scott snapped a piece of shortbread in two as the caramel strung out between the two pieces before snapping to drip down the back of his hand. "Someone needs to drag him off there."

"We could take him." Tommy glared over his shoulder at the bar. "He's barely out of boot camp, and you—"

"Don't say it in here." The last thing he wanted was a bunch of freshly minted seamen knowing what he did for a living. He wasn't in the mood for war stories tonight. "He's on the final chorus, so maybe he'll shut up and give some other asshole a chance."

"I wasn't going to say it in here." Tommy glared at him. "I'm offended that you think I'd ever mention it in public unless you did first."

"Well, there was that time..."

"Asshole." Tommy grinned at him. "Man, you need to come home more often. It's not the same around here without you."

"You mean there's no rubber being burned all the way down East Scranton to the park every Friday night?" Scott chimed in. "Sheriff McKay retired about six months ago. I think he got bored when he didn't have us to chase around town."

"Jeez." Kentucky clenched his fists when the asshole on stage didn't leave when he was done butchering Bon Jovi. "That fucker thinks he's all that and a bag of chips."

"Get off the damn stage!" someone yelled from the other side of the room.

"Can I beat him?" a man just a little down for them asked. "Please, let me at least throw something at him."

Damn it, the patrons were getting noticeably pissed. If Kentucky didn't defuse the situation with some smartass comment soon, there would be problems his ma didn't need. He cupped his hand around his mouth and yelled toward the stage, "Hey, Mozart, get off the stage and let someone else slaughter a song for a while." The whole bar erupted in laughter and howls of delight. As much as Kentucky hated being the one to cause a scene, especially in here, he was as relieved as everyone else in the bar when the seaman's buddies went and dragged him off the stage. Good, if the worst that lanky kid got out of tonight was a nickname, then he'd be just fine.

"Mozart. Fucking epic." Scott refilled his glass from the bottle of Knob's Creek. "Here, throw that down your neck."

"Thanks." Kentucky tossed it back and relished the burn. But before he could place the glass back on the counter to be refilled, his pager buzzed in his pocket. "Damn." He pulled it out and glanced at the number. "I gotta go." He didn't need to make the call to know he was on standby for a mission. "I gotta get back to Virginia."

"Damn, man, you just got here."

"I know, T. I'll be back though, I promise." He didn't give a shit that he was standing in the middle of his mother's bar. He hugged both of them. "Stay out of trouble and look after my ma."

"Always, bro."

Now he just had to tell his mother his leave had been pulled, and he was going back to work. He hated upsetting her, but thankfully, she understood how important his job was. Hell, she'd lived the life with his father before they'd retired and come back here to take over the bar her family had owned forever. It had sucked when they'd had to buy it off the bank because her brother had been more fond of betting on horses than he had been on paying the bills. But they'd made it work, even when his dad hadn't been able to deal with the nightmares anymore and had eaten a bullet in the storage shed out back. "I'll see you when I see you." He tapped his fingers to the bill of his ball cap and slipped behind the bar just as his pager buzzed again.

"You're leaving."

He should have known his mother would figure out why he wasn't still in the bar drinking. And even though it wasn't a question, he answered her as if it were. "Yes, Ma, I'm going back to work."

She smiled softly at him, and he could tell she'd swallowed down a sigh. "I'll pack you some food."

"Thank you. I'll be down to hug you in a minute." He turned toward the door which led to their private quarters, but paused and smiled over his shoulder. "I love you, Ma."

"I love you, too."

CHAPTER ONE

Twelve years later. San Diego CA

KENTUCKY TAPPED the address into the GPS and peered at it. He pinched the screen a couple of times to zoom it out so he could see where it was in relation to her house. Good, he was only a couple of streets away. He was probably way overstepping the mark by coming down here to visit Becky, and definitely was overstepping by not calling to check if he could visit or not, never mind bring the boys with him.

But there wasn't a chance in hell he wasn't visiting her. He needed to see she was okay. Giving her the option to say 'no, she wasn't up to visitors today' had seemed like an awesome idea when he'd left Riverton. Now he wasn't so sure. But she'd adapt, she was stronger than she knew. From the second he'd pulled her out of that hellhole she'd been in, along with Cormack's woman, her strength and resilience had awed him. But he also knew better than most, even the strongest oak will crack given enough pressure. Her voice on the phone the last couple of times he'd spoken to her had been—off—he didn't know how else to describe it—her voice was just off. She would just have to deal with his happy ass checking on her.

Spending the last few days with Wolf Steel and his team had been awesome, but he craved the solitude which came with the mountains. Now that his second in command, Rexar, had found Lily and his son, maybe he could take the downtime he needed and find somewhere to get to know Becky a little better. Maybe now she'd had some time to come to terms with what had happened to her, she'd be ready to see him as more than a friend.

Stop it, you idiot. You know better than to hope or wish for stuff. Every time you do, everything goes to hell in a handbasket.

"I'm too old for this shit." He steered the truck down streets lined with houses, each one decorated for Christmas more elaborately than the last. "Jeez, you could see every one of these places from the space station." He turned his head slightly to the right to avoid the glare from one house. "They will cause a freaking accident. How the hell can those blue flashing lights be legal? They almost look like a cop car."

"Yeah, they're kinda over the top, aren't they?" Draven bumped him with his elbow when he shifted in his seat. "My pop would yell about the cost of the electric bill, for sure."

"So would my ma." While his mom loved Christmas, she also preferred her bills marked as paid. Even with the bar, there was no way she'd have this many lights going, and she'd be turning them off once the bar closed for sure. These people either didn't have to worry about the bills or they had exactly zero common sense. He was tempted to think it was the latter.

"I think she's just up here on the left." Draven pointed to a side street. "About six houses in from the street exit."

Kentucky glanced at the GPS to double-check. It wouldn't be the first time Draven Kilkenny got them lost by 'thinking' they were meant to go in a certain direction. This time, however, his teammate was spot on. "Yep." Just as they took the turn, movement up ahead caught his eye, and he tapped on the brakes, then whipped the truck to the side and parked next to the pavement in front of a house. Every internal warning signal he had fired into life. You didn't spend most of your life in troubled hotspots across the globe and not learn when to pay attention. For the record, he was definitely paying attention now. "Do you see that?"

"Weird." Draven leaned forward as if being five inches closer to the windshield would allow him to see the movement of the vehicles up ahead better. "Are those unmarked law enforcement vehicles?"

"Sure looks like it, doesn't it?" Kentucky watched as one dark sedan pulled out of a parking space and stopped to talk to a similar style vehicle before driving off. The other car took the parking spot the first had been parked in. "Get me Trev on the line. I want to know if we are walking into a situation." His guts screamed at him to hurry. He needed to get to Becky right now. But damn, his fucking years of experience and lessons he'd learned the hard way ensured he didn't take off running—or driving, as the case would be tonight.

"On it."

Kentucky kept his eyes on the scene in front of him. He ran multiple scenarios through his mind as to why unmarked police cars would be parked across from Becky's house and not one of those scenarios were ones he liked. He drummed his fingers on the steering wheel as he waited for the phone to connect.

"Hey, Trev," Draven said next to him. "I'm putting you on speaker. Ken needs to talk to you."

"What's wrong?" Their communication and intel expert's

voice was gravelly, as if he'd just woken up from a deep sleep. "I thought you were gonna go visit Miss. B?"

"I am," Kentucky replied. "I'm parked just down the street from her place and watched what looks like LEOs do a handover, and it's news to me that they are watching her house. Is there something I need to know?"

"If there is, I don't know about it either. It shouldn't take me long to find out, though. And if I can't, then we know Tex has contacts in the area. I can ask him to take a look." The sound of shuffling sheets filtered over the phone, followed by a whispered, "Go back to sleep. I have to go to work."

Shit.

Had Trev finally taken a day off and they'd disturbed him? If so, Dalton wouldn't be thrilled about it. He'd been trying to get their comms tech to take time off for years. Kentucky winced at the twinge of guilt he felt, but pushed it aside. Becky was more important than anyone's day off, even Trev's. "Sorry, bro..."

"No, you're fine," Trev cut him off. "I needed to get back anyway. Give me ten minutes and I'll call you back." The screen went dark as Trev ended the call. Wherever he was, Trev couldn't be too far from the war room. There was no freaking way he could make it back onto the ranch from town in ten minutes. Which meant he had to be with someone on the ranch.

Interesting.

"Did you catch that?" For all of his problems with his sense of direction, Draven was pretty quick on the uptake for most other things.

"Yeah, it sounded like he was with someone." Since the changeover of the unmarked cars, nothing moved near Becky's house that he could see. He was tempted to just drive on up there. He glanced at his watch. Shit, at ten PM at night, maybe he should have thought to call ahead. But he'd been concerned she'd say no. Damn it. He didn't like this second-guessing shit at all.

"Do you think it was Snow?" Caleb leaned between the front seats. "That Trev was with, I mean? If it was, I'm telling Braddock just so I can see shit and feathers fly."

To be fair, it was a reasonable assumption as Aria *Snow* Keane, Alpha Team's sniper, was one of the few unattached women at Nemesis ranch. "If it was," Kentucky tapped Caleb on the side of the head, "you won't say jack shit. Do you really want to find yourself on the wrong side of Snow's sniper rifle? That's just stupid. Sit your ass back in that seat and hit reinstall on your brain cells as there's a malfunction somewhere."

"But, man… Braddock would lose his shit," Caleb replied. "That could totally be fun to watch."

"Hell, no he wouldn't," Bryan *BB* Boyer chimed in. "He'd sit his ass down and place bets on how fast his spitfire cousin could rip you a new one."

Kentucky knew their bickering and teasing was a way to keep him distracted and in place while they waited for Trev to get his butt in the chair at his computers. Kentucky had been around the block too many times to not be able to read the men he was almost as close to as he was Tommy and Scott, his best buds from when he was a kid. He understood it, appreciated it even. But it still chaffed at him. He did not want to be sitting here fucking waiting. He stared down the street, his eyes moving from that vehicle to Becky's house and back again. Cops didn't just park themselves up for nothing. They had to be there for a reason.

"Stop it, old man." As if Draven picked up on the effort it was taking him to stay in place, he punched him on the arm. "Trev will tell you if there is a threat in a couple of minutes. Don't make yourself cray-cray until then."

"We could just drive up there and park our happy asses in her driveway..."

"As much as I'd fucking love to do that, I don't dare," Kentucky cut BB off. "Because if something bad enough to have LEOs watching her place has happened, I don't want to scare the pants off her."

"I'm sure scaring the pants off her isn't how you intend on getting them off—"

Normally, Kentucky considered himself fairly level-headed. In the jobs they did, he had to be, and he'd long ago learned how to keep a harness on his temper. But as he heard the words coming out of BB's mouth, he saw colors in his head... most of them were red. In a flash, he was leaning over the seat, his fingers fisted into BB's shirt, and he yanked him forward until they were nose to nose. "Shut your damn mouth. You will show her fucking respect, or you will answer to me. Do you understand?"

"Yes, Sir."

BB had probably been trash talking, just as he normally did, but Kentucky didn't care. "She is off limits for your smack talking. If you ever speak like that about her again, you are going to be on a redeye to one of the 'Stans before you finish speaking. Do you understand me?" He knew Dalton would back his call if it came down to it. It wouldn't be the first time they'd sent someone back overseas for some infraction or other. Usually to get the asshole involved out of their sight, so they weren't tempted to use him for target practice.

"I'm sorry." BB winced and patted Kentucky's shoulder. "I was joking around. It was in bad taste. I promise I'll engage my brain and keep the shit talk to a minimum."

Every single one of them snorted at the promise. Bryan may have good intentions, but he wasn't blessed with a mouth which could restrain itself from shit talk.

"Boss, there's something happening." Draven's words defused the situation as quickly as it has escalated, and they all snapped into work mode.

Kentucky whipped his head around to the front just in time to see two men running flat out across the street toward Becky's house. He slammed his idling truck into gear and aimed its nose toward her driveway. "I'm coming, Becks."

Jesus, please let her be okay.

He shouldn't have waited here for Trev to get back to his desk. He should have gone straight up there. He was a fucking idiot.

Please let her be okay.

CHAPTER TWO

Trying to sleep was freaking useless. Even with all the lights in the house on, it was impossible. Every time Becky closed her eyes, all she could see was the shipping container cell she'd been held in for way too long. Or worse, the rooms she'd been taken to when the men who held her decided they wanted to be entertained.

"This is ridiculous." She flipped back the covers and swung her legs over the edge of her bed. She was hearing things now, because she knew there was no way that thump could have come from her house. There was a police car right across the street, for God's sake. Someone would have to be an idiot to try to break in here. But she could not get past the feeling of ice sliding down the back of her neck and she needed to check the house again, or she'd never be able to rest.

She unlocked the bedroom door and padded down the hallway toward the kitchen. Maybe some tea would help. "Did the bulb blow?" She paused in the hallway just before the kitchen. She'd left the lights on when she'd gone to bed. She was certain of it. She never turned the lights off, not even during the daytime, as she couldn't bear the thought of snoozing on the couch and waking in darkness. She'd spent enough time in the dark.

Just reach in and flip on the switch. It's right there inside the door.

You are being a ninny. Turn on the fricking light.

Becky swallowed hard. She could do this. It was just reaching her hand around the door for heaven's sake. It was right there. She reached out with her hand; her fingers shook more than they should. But there was no way she was going to be beaten by the dark. Logically, she knew the dark alone couldn't hurt her. But…

Just do it.

She fully expected some boogeyman to grab her hand when she reached around and patted the wall until they skimmed over the switch cover, and she flipped down the switch. When the kitchen flooded with light, she wanted to smack herself for being silly. She must have flipped it off when she'd left the room earlier. Probably because of some long-instilled reflex from before everything had changed in her world.

She crossed the room to the sink and grabbed the electric kettle Willow had sent here with her from Montana and filled it at the sink. Why hadn't she thought to buy one of these for making tea before? It was so much faster than waiting for a pot or a kettle to boil on the stovetop. She put it back on its base and flipped down the button to set it to boil. "Tea? Which tea am I having?" She opened the drawer where she'd stashed the gifts Kentucky kept sending her. She flipped through the little envelopes of tea bags. "Every flavor known to man, and I have to choose just one." She picked up two and held one in each hand. "Chamomile or lemon and ginger? Decisions, decisions."

How on earth was one supposed to decide when her

mind kept tumbling and jumbling over everything? She placed them on the counter and opened the cupboard over her head for an insulated tumbler. "Making both would be a ridiculous waste." She closed her eyes and felt for the tea bags on the counter. Whichever one her hand touched first was the one she'd use. When her fingers brushed off paper, she picked it up and peered at the packet. "Chamomile it is."

The click of the kettle switching off made her jump. "It's a normal sound, damn it. Act normal about it." She dropped the tea bag into the mug and filled it with hot water. After making sure the label hung over the rim, she screwed the top on. With how much she was jumping at shadows, she didn't dare use a China cup or even a mug, because she'd drop it and burn herself for sure.

Once she'd unplugged the kettle, she picked up her tumbler of tea and turned around. It only took a second for her eyes to land on the item which was out of place. She froze as the mug slipped through her fingers and bounced on the tile floor.

"Nooo!" she screamed, dropped to the floor, and scooted backward on her butt until she was in a spot with her back to the wall. She felt under the kitchen cabinet for the kitchen knife she'd put there. Her 'just in case I'm cornered' safety net. Her emergency weapon to fight back with. She may be jumpy—her nerves were having a damn party—but she was determined she was never going back to the situation she'd been in before. Ever.

How had they found her? This couldn't be possible. Even the police had tried to convince her she was crazy when she'd gone to the station the day before yesterday. Heck, she thought she was losing her mind. The notes and the presents left on her doorstep couldn't possibly be connected to the ordeal, as she called it, she went through. But there was no way this was a figment of her imagination. "They've been in my house. Oh my god. They've been in my house."

She knew she wasn't meant to tell anyone how she'd been rescued, or even that she'd been taken in the first place, so she'd glossed over it as much as she could with the police. But how did you explain a bunch of commandos had rescued her from a sex trafficker? She also didn't mention one of those commandos was now the husband of a woman held with her. But it had been impossible to get the police to take her seriously when she couldn't give them many details. She'd figured out a way to convince them she had a stalker. She'd promised Kentucky and Nemesis Inc. that she'd keep her mouth shut to protect not only Willow Black-Ford but her own reputation. If she ever wanted to go back to teaching, she couldn't have this kind of stain on her records.

But she couldn't live in fear anymore. The shackles which had just been left on her kitchen counter confirmed whoever was hunting her had been in her house.

You should call Ken. He'll come.

She could call him. She should have told him when he'd called her a couple of days ago. But Kentucky was hours away in Montana. He'd done enough to help her. She couldn't ask him for more. She sucked in a shaky breath and blew it out slowly. Sooner or later, she had to start dealing with things herself instead of relying on the hot swoony former SEAL to come running to her rescue.

She stared at the shackles as if it was a snake which would strike out and bite her. She pressed herself into the corner between the wall and the fridge. Maybe if she squeezed her eyes closed tight enough, when she opened them, she'd find this had all been a dream.

A thump further into the house scared the last of any wits she had out of her. She slapped one hand over her mouth to prevent the scream she could feel building from escaping and she pressed the big red button on the alarm necklace one of the female cops had been kind enough to give her. She'd been so grateful to have it she hadn't even cared, it was a medical emergency alert alarm most typically used by the elderly.

She'd seen the unmarked car parked across from her house when she'd looked earlier. But she didn't know how long they would be there or even if they were still there or not. The police had promised once they had to leave that patrol cars would drive by multiple times over the next few days. That alone had told her, while they'd tried to play down her concerns, they had enough concern about a stalker to make sure she was protected.

Please still be there. Please still be there. Please still be there.

What felt like a lifetime later was probably little more than a minute, and Becky cringed back into her corner when a loud hammering sounded at the door.

Oh, god.

"Police. Police, open up."

What were they waiting for, a freaking invitation? They knew she had a stalker. She'd hit the freaking alarm. Why weren't they coming right on in? She pressed the button again, over and over.

"Police. You have ten seconds and we're coming in."

"Ten seconds. I could be dead in ten seconds."

The sound of footsteps running toward the back of her house confirmed there was someone in the house. She wasn't imagining it. She screamed when a massive bang sounded and her front door slammed open.

"Police, hands in the air. Hands in the air." The first one through the door made a beeline for her. "Get on the ground, get on the ground. Put the knife down, put the weapon down. Now."

Why was he screaming at her? She dropped the kitchen knife on the floor. But there wasn't a chance in hell that she was lying down. She was already almost curled into a ball. That would just have to be enough.

"That's our vic, dumbass." The older cop elbowed the one screaming at her out of the way. "Clear the damn house."

"I—I heard someone running that way," she hiccupped and pointed down the hallway toward the bedroom. "I didn't see him."

"Are you okay, Ma'am?" The policeman stood with his weapon trained on the hallway as the other one carefully worked his way down toward the bedroom. "We've got you. You're safe."

He could say that all he wanted. She didn't feel safe. She never felt safe. She pointed toward the shackles on her counter when a voice called her name. "They left that. It's not mine. I—"

"Becky?"

"Ken." She scrambled to her feet and shot around the cop, making a beeline toward the door. Even the sight of a weapon in Kentucky's hand didn't stop her.

"Put your weapons down!" the cop screamed behind her. "Lower your weapons."

She ran full pelt across her kitchen and living room to where Kentucky stepped to one side of the door and another man she recognized but whose name she couldn't remember took his place.

"Brace, bro," the second man warned Kentucky a split second before she launched herself into his arms.

"I got you. I got you."

She wrapped her legs around his waist as he spun them around so his back was to the room and hers against the wall. Somehow, the words he kept repeating meant safety. The policeman had used the same words only a couple of seconds before, but they had been meaningless. These ones meant everything.

"Take care of that shit." Kentucky adjusted his hands under her butt, making sure she was secure in his hold. "And keep that cop away from me. I get kinda jumpy when someone is pointing a weapon at my back."

"On it, Boss."

One hand rubbed up and down her back, gentle but firm. "And someone call Nem, Mozart, and Commander Hurt. Stat."

"I've got it," another voice from someone Becky couldn't see past Kentucky's bulk chimed in. "BB's on your six."

"Copy."

With her face buried in Kentucky's neck, she couldn't see who was who or what was happening. But did she need to see? No. No, she didn't. She knew he'd fix it. "I'm scared."

"Shh, baby, I got you." Kentucky shifted her in his arms. "Are you hurt? Do I need to an ambulance or a doctor?"

She shook her head, because now that her body had finally realized she was safe, she could feel the hysteria building inside her.

"Words, baby, I'm gonna need words."

His soft southern drawl washed over her. She bunched her hands into his shirt, clutching at his back. If he made her stand, she wasn't sure her legs would hold her just yet. "I—I'm okay. Just scared."

"I got you. I promise."

CHAPTER THREE

"Stand down, sir," a voice Kentucky was going to assume belonged to the cop he'd glimpsed just before Becky had barreled into him said.

"I'm sorry, I can't do that until we have verified who you are."

Kentucky stiffened when he heard Bryan speak behind his right shoulder. Thankfully, his team understood they weren't to take any chances with Becky's safety. It wouldn't be the first time a criminal had posed as a cop to get close to their target. He didn't dare move in case the cop got trigger-happy. At least with Becky wrapped in his arms and his body between her and the rest of the house, to get to her, someone would have to go through him and his team. Period. The more she trembled and shook in fear, the more his rage built. He breathed in harshly through his nose and let it out slowly. "What happened, baby?"

"Counter, kitchen."

His heart cracked at the wobble in her voice.

"Bravo Five, check the kitchen counter." Let the cop think they were still military. Nemesis would have to figure out how to smooth shit over later on. "Becks said there's something on it."

"Don't touch whatever it is!" BB yelled immediately when he finished speaking.

"I'm not an idiot," Caleb answered. "Boss, there's a damn set of shackles like..."

His voice trailed off, allowing Kentucky to fill in the blanks. It didn't take a freaking rocket scientist to know what his teammate meant. The shackles were like the ones they'd cut off Becky and Willow when they'd rescued them a few months ago. He swallowed down the bile and rage. She didn't need him over the top, losing his shit right now. He strove for a calm he didn't feel, and finding any sort of calm wasn't likely to happen for at least the next ten years at this rate. "Fuck."

"I came down to make tea. I couldn't sleep," Becky whispered against his neck. "I kept hearing the house make noise. You know, the creaking and settling houses do at night." She waited for his nod before she continued. "I kept imagining I was seeing shadows move, and I thought tea would help settle my nerves."

"That's when you saw it?"

"No, I flipped on the lights. They were off. I never turn them off. I thought maybe the bulb had blown," she explained. "I made tea, and when I turned back around, they were there. I panicked. I'm sorry."

"Baby, you have nothing to be sorry for." He rubbed the side of his face on the top of her head. "They weren't there when you walked into the kitchen?"

He felt her shake her head against his neck, and reality slammed into him. The bastard had been close enough to put the fucking shackles on the counter less than five feet from her. He was close enough to take her.

Fuck.

Fuck.

He squeezed his arms a little tighter around her and sighed in relief when she didn't stiffen, but snuggled in closer. "Unless you put those shackles on your counter, which I highly doubt, then there was someone in this house." He turned his head slightly and glared at the cop out of the corner of his eye. "You are supposed to be fucking protecting her, right? Where the hell were you when that asshole was breaking in here?"

"Man, we just came on shift," the other cop spluttered. "The previous shift said all was quiet." He'd apparently figured out that Ken and his team weren't the bad guys in this situation.

"We saw your change over." He decided it couldn't hurt to let the cops know he'd been watching them. He wanted to see if they'd noticed they had an audience.

"You did?"

Kentucky snorted. That answered that question. "Jesus, you aren't very fucking observant, are you?" He didn't care how many toes he stepped on. His happy ass was going down to the police station and he would tell them how freaking incompetent they were. "We stopped at the end of the street, and you didn't even see us. What if we were the people after my woman?" He ignored the sting when this time Becky stiffened in his arms as he called her his.

But enough of this being separate shit. She'd wanted, no, she'd insisted she needed time to process and figure out where she'd wanted her life to go. He'd agreed because he wasn't an asshole, and he hadn't known she was still in danger. He should have known better than to trust when something had been touched by fucking King and The Organization that she'd ever be safe.

She'd be safe in Montana.

Yes. Yes, she would.

"The big boss is onto the chief of police." Draven elbowed the cop out of the way and approached them. "He's on his way."

"Alpha One is on his way?"

"Nope, the chief of police is coming here now," Draven corrected. "Mozart, Benny, and possibly T-Rex are on their way, too. Alpha One will be wheels up ASAP."

"Fuck. T-Rex needs to look after his family. He just got them back." If it was for anyone else but Becky, he'd feel so damn guilty about pulling Rexar away from Lily and RJ. But for her. To protect her, he'd swallow every ounce of pride he had and call in every chip he was owed.

"Good luck with telling him that shit, bro," BB snorted. "T-Rex will come on the run for brothers every damn time and twice on a Sunday."

"Yeah." He couldn't really bitch about it when he'd do exactly the same thing. He shifted his arm under Becky's ass, and she tightened her arms and legs around him. Clearly, she wasn't ready to be on her feet yet. Now he was sure the cops were actually cops and not a threat, he scanned the room. "I'm just gonna sit us on the couch."

"I'm too heavy." She sounded mortified and immediately pushed against him and dropped her legs from his waist.

"The hell you are, baby." He refused to let her go. He needed to hold her just a little longer, to reassure himself she was safe. "If you keep struggling, Imma gonna be writing it into my notebook to remind me we need to have a discussion about you putting yourself down."

"Jeez, Ma'am. Don't make him bring out the notebook," Caleb quipped. "I'm still working off infractions from the last time that thing made an appearance."

One of those infractions was going to be scratched off with no extra laps required during PT. His brothers in arms were busy doing their best to help make her comfortable. "I want a team here…" Now that he'd turned them away from the wall, he could look the cops in their eyes. "I want those shackles bagged as evidence, and I want every inch of this house, internal and external, fingerprinted."

"That's not—"

"I don't give a fuck what it is or isn't." He knew his voice was cold and angry. But he couldn't bring himself to give one shit about it, never mind two. "You will do it, if only because your asses weren't on the ball when they should have been. That fucker could have taken her, and you'd never have known it and just considered yourselves lucky that 'all was quiet.'" He scoffed the last words. He settled himself into the couch, but kept Becky on his lap. There wasn't a chance in hell he was letting her out of his arms. Even if she didn't need him, he needed her there to remind him she was alive, breathing, and he was right here, where he could protect her.

A sharp knock at the door and every single one of his team had their weapons raised to ready position, despite the protests of the two cops.

"What the hell is going on in here?" The man dressed in a suit who entered raised both his hands. "I'm Chief Dunn."

Draven glanced at him, and Kentucky nodded. "Let him in."

"You." Chief Dunn pointed to him and moved closer, only to find himself blocked by a wall of pissed off mercs. "Jesus, assholes, I won't hurt him." He cocked his head to one side and glanced at Kentucky and Becky again. "Or her," he added on. "He's the one you are all deferring to, so I'm guessing he's the one I need to talk to."

"Did my boss call you?" Kentucky once again nodded to the guys. He appreciated how protective his guys were of them. He mentally scratched items off the list in his notebook. Just as soon as he had Becky somewhere safe, he'd do that scratching for real.

"If your boss is Dalton Knight, then yes, he did." The chief of police came closer, but after a glance at the team, decided he didn't need to be right next to the couch after all. "I have investigators on the way. As soon as they get here, I'm going to need you all to come down to the station."

"Our legal team is on the way, too." Kentucky didn't need to put a call into HQ to know this was true. Every time the police were involved with anything related to them, Dalton would have Riga Bishop on the next flight from South Carolina. "Until they arrive, we aren't talking."

"What he said," Becky chimed in. God bless her for backing him up without having been coached to do so.

"We already have your report on file, Rebecca...."

"That's Ms. Jones to you," Kentucky snapped. If the cops or even the chief of police thought by being familiar that they'd leave their guard down, then they had another think coming. "Our legal team will need to have a copy of that report, too." He didn't even care that the chief of police's jaw tightened. The man needed to understand that someone got close to her on their fucking watch. It was their freaking responsibility to fix it and make sure she was safe.

Hell no. I'm not leaving a bunch of Muppets to look after her. She's coming home with me.

But he knew that was a hell of a lot easier said than done. She had to agree to come. He wouldn't force her. She'd been forced enough over the months she'd been in captivity, and he wouldn't be the one to put her in that position again. But she'd have to figure out fast when it came to her safety, he wasn't taking any more chances. Period.

CHAPTER FOUR

This could not be happening. She had done everything right. She'd been careful. She didn't use social media. The only people she spoke to on the phone were Kentucky and Willow. She'd never been close to her family. She wasn't even sure she would recognize her own mother if she passed her on the street. "Why does this keep happening to me?" She didn't want to go to the station again. It hadn't been the most pleasant experience the last time.

"I don't know, baby." Kentucky ignored the chief of police and leaned down to whisper softly in her ear. "But it stops right now. Because I won't stop until I fix this shit."

She was meant to be a modern woman and able to do everything herself. But just this once, she wanted to burrow underneath his shirt and stay there. Kentucky would growl and grumble at everyone but her. Which should be scary to her, but it wasn't as she knew he'd keep the scary things away and keep her safe.

But what if he gets hurt because of you?

Don't be stupid. Do you not remember what he's like in action? GI Joe should take notes. Lots of notes.

"I know." Now that she had time to soak in some of the warmth which seemed to radiate off Kentucky, she could feel the fear receding. It was absolutely ridiculous that it took sitting on his lap for her to find what remained of her marbles. "Just don't make me do it alone."

"Boss, Bravo Two and co are coming in hot," the one she thought might be Draven called from where he stood at her front door.

"Let him in."

She didn't need to wonder who Bravo Two was, as within seconds, he filled the front door. This man she also recognized from her time in Montana. He was Willow's uncle, or at least a pseudo uncle. She didn't know the men who followed him in, though. But she if she had to guess by the chin lift Kentucky gave them, he knew these people, and that was good enough for her.

"The one behind Rexar," Kentucky whispered in her ear, "is your landlord. I know you know his name. But for now, call him Mozart, okay?"

"Okay."

"The other man is Benny. He works with Mozart."

She didn't need him to tell her Benny was a SEAL. She remembered Kentucky telling her the man who owned her house was one, just like he had been before he'd gone to work with Nemesis Inc. If Benny worked with Mozart, then logic said Benny was a SEAL, too.

Mozart glanced at her and Kentucky. "Are you okay, Becky?"

"Yes, I am now." She was so freaking proud of herself that her voice didn't shake as much as it wanted to. She figured the tiny bit it wobbled was more than understandable, given the circumstances.

"Who are you?" The chief of police snapped his finger to draw Mozart's attention.

Becky was fascinated when Mozart's face switched from concern when he'd spoken to her, to completely blank just before he spun around to answer the chief.

"I'm Mozart." Even his voice was cold. "I own this house."

"Unless you are involved in this situation, you have no reason to be here," the chief decided. "As landlord, you have access to keys, and therefore, access to the property." He turned to the other cops and pointed to Mozart. "Cuff him and take him downtown."

"Hey. It's not him." There was no way she was allowing this bully to be an asshole to her friends.

"It's okay, Becky," Mozart said. "It's S.O.P, and I expected this to happen."

"S.O.P.?" She was going to need a dictionary if they started talking in anagrams like most of the guys had in Montana. "I'm going to need words, not riddles."

"S.O.P. is Standard Operating Procedure," Kentucky said quietly. "The police need to be sure."

"You don't think—"

He pressed his finger to her lips, stopping the question before she could finish it. "Hell no, Mozart just drove down from Riverton with T-Rex and Benny. There is no way he made it here before me, because I left him there before we hit the road."

"Good." It was so easy to find her big girl panties and pull them on while sitting here safe on Kentucky's lap. "Officer—"

"Chief Dunn." The asshole apparently didn't have a momma who taught him any manners. "It's not Mozart." She barely remembered to use the name he'd given to the snooty ass. "If it was, there is no way he'd still be standing as my—Kentucky—" she stumbled again but forced herself to keep going. Hopefully they all would think it was trauma, and not because they thought she was calling Kentucky hers, "—would have put him through the wall the second he stepped into the house. Plus, he'd never have suggested this house as a safe place for me to land if he had any doubt about his friend." If she put a little extra emphasis on the word friend, then it was totally intentional.

"We have to eliminate all suspects."

"It's okay." Mozart allowed them to cuff him. "We'll get this cleared up pretty quick once we get to the precinct downtown."

"I'm sorry, man," Kentucky said.

"Nah," Mozart cut him off. "I just gotta call Commander Hurt and he'll sort it."

"Mozart, are you taking my name in vain?" Another man entered the house, followed by a couple of others who looked similar to the people who did all the fingerprinting and stuff on TV shows. This man commanded authority and even the chief of police seemed to stand straighter and pay attention when he spoke. "What's going on here?" He glanced around the room, scowled at the policemen, then nodded to her and Kentucky. "I want an explanation now."

"This lady's house was broken into," the chief of police said. "Your man." He paused and pointed at Mozart. "I'm assuming he's your man?"

"He is," the commander growled. "Get on with it."

"He has access to the property. He's a suspect."

"This is just a ridiculous comedy of errors. Mozart hurting a woman… if you'd even looked into him, you'd know that's never gonna happen," Commander Hurt grumbled. "Do we need to go downtown, or can we handle this here?"

"Downtown."

"Fabulous." The commander twirled one finger in the air. "Then get moving. I don't have all day to sit around watching your people look for their elbow in their ass."

"Yes, Sir."

"We're waiting on Riga Bishop arriving from South Carolina," Kentucky said. "You know Riga, don't you, Sir?"

"Yes, I do." Commander Hurt grinned at Kentucky and winked at her. "I know him. Served with him, and if he's coming, he can pay me the fifty bucks he owes me."

Kentucky stood off the couch and carefully put her on her feet. He laced his fingers with hers, and Becky smiled up at him. She should have known he wouldn't let her walk out the door all by herself.

"Hah, you're just going around collecting debts," Rexar spoke for the first time. "It's good to see you again, sir."

"How's that family of yours, T-Rex?" Commander Hurt shook the hand Rexar extended to him.

"Good, sir, thank you for asking." Rexar's entire face lit up when he was asked about his family. "My boy is a chip off the old block."

"I saw that." The commander and Rexar followed them out the door. "I'll meet you all downtown." He tossed Rexar a set of keys. "I'm going to ride with Mozart."

A chorus of 'yes, sirs' followed his statement.

Becky found herself sandwiched between the guys as they moved from the house to a big black truck. "Caleb, you're driving," Kentucky ordered. "BB, you're with T-Rex, and, Draven, you have shotgun for us."

"Copy that."

"You got it, Boss."

"Yes, sir."

They all scattered, and before she knew it, Kentucky was helping her into the back of the closest truck before he slid in next to her.

"I didn't want you squished back here with the guys."

"Thank you." She might have been able to deal with

having someone else on the other side of her. But now that it was only herself and Kentucky, she knew it wouldn't have been the most comfortable ride to the station.

"It's all good, doll." Kentucky ran his thumb over the back of her hand. "We wouldn't want to scare those jackasses by having them sit next to you." He shifted on the seat, almost leaning over her to reach into his ass pocket. He pulled out a notebook and waved it under her nose. "They wouldn't want to end up with another mark to their name, or they'll be running laps until at least Christmas next year, never mind this year."

She knew what he was doing... distracting her... giving her a second to breathe and find her equilibrium with all the changes happening. While she appreciated it, she couldn't figure out why he didn't know that around him she was as balanced as she was ever going to get.

"Please don't make him add more notes to the book." Caleb reversed out of her driveway before putting the truck in gear and following the car Rexar and BB and gotten into. "I have enough marks against my name. I'm going to need someone to gift me some running shoes for Christmas."

"I'm not that bad." Kentucky fumbled in another pocket and produced a pen, then flipped open his notebook.

From where she sat next to him, she could see him crossing out lines of code she couldn't understand. When she glanced up at him, Kentucky was peering over the rim of the notebook, making eye contact with Draven as he worked the pen across the page as if he was making a notation. He was teasing them, and they didn't even know it. She leaned to his ear and whispered, "You big faker."

"I promise you, doll. Faking isn't something I excel at."

"Hmm."

"I'll prove it to you at some point," he promised. "No faking needed."

Even she caught the innuendo in his voice, and dang it, sister, if it didn't send a shiver right through her. The corners of her lips curved upward and before she could stop herself, the words popped out of her mouth. "Bring it, Tuck."

CHAPTER FIVE

Tuck? She's shortening my name. I like that. Nope, scratch the like. I fucking love that she's doing that.

Kentucky's eyes widened at her words. Did she even know what she was doing to him? He didn't think so. He smiled down at Becky's sparkling eyes. He was so freaking relieved what had happened hadn't killed her spirit. He knew there was a feisty woman in there. She just needed to feel safe enough to allow that woman in her soul to shine.

"We're here," Caleb announced.

Fan-freaking-tastic. I'm gonna be walking into the cop shop with a fucking hard-on.

He didn't dare adjust the tightness of his pants though, because doing so might shove the glimpses he was seeing of the real Becky back behind the wall she typically hid behind. He cleared his throat. "You ready for this?" he asked Becky.

"No, and I really don't want to do this." She laid her head on his shoulder. "But I'll do it anyway, because I don't want Mozart or any of you in trouble for longer than you have to be."

She'd do it for them and not for herself. He wasn't sure if

he was proud of her for her resilience or if he should be all kinds of upset that she still wasn't putting herself first. She'd more than earned the right to consider herself before everyone else. "I'll be with you every step of the way," he promised. Draven got out and opened the door for them. "Let's do this, doll. It's time to remind them who they are dealing with."

"GI Joe." She took his hand and allowed him to help her out of the truck. "Multiple GI Joes."

"No, Ma'am," Draven piped up before Kentucky could. "We ain't no GI Joes, we have…"

Kentucky scowled at his teammate. He had no freaking clue what Draven had been about to say, but he knew by the way the asshole had cut off his words that he'd figured out it probably wasn't something he should say in the presence of a lady.

"GI Joe doesn't have what?" Becky nudged him with her elbow, giving him a heads up… she was okay with the teasing.

I'm so fucking proud of her.

"Do tell, Kilkenny." There was no freaking way he was letting this opportunity to fuck with Draven pass him by. "I can't wait to hear this."

"I… ah—"

"Saved by the door," Becky said as Rexar held the door to the police station open for them. "Because I'm guessing what you were about to say wasn't exactly fit for public consumption."

"Damn straight." Draven sounded relieved.

Kentucky decided he would let him get away with it. His doll face wasn't walking in the door with her shoulders slumped and fear in her eyes. He'd take it every damn day and twice on a Sunday.

"Separate them all," the chief of police ordered.

"Hell no." He understood the logic behind the order, and he also understood procedures and shit. But separating from Becky wasn't happening. "I stay with Becky. Period."

"That is not how this is going to work, Mr..."

"Bravo One." He snapped out his call sign. Until Riga Bishop's butt was here on the ground, he wasn't budging from Becky's side. "I do not give you my name. If you needed to know it, my boss would have given it to you while you were talking to him on the phone."

"It's okay," Becky whispered.

He figured she probably didn't realize how he could feel her fingers trembling in his. "No, it's not. Until we have legal representation, or they arrest us, they will not separate us."

"Ar—arrest us?" She narrowed her eyes at the policeman. "Why on earth would they arrest us? I'm the one whose house got broken into."

"Right."

This shit right here was one of the reasons he worked black jobs in countries they probably shouldn't be in. There was no need for following rules and nobody aside from Dalton or Trev to... even as he had the thought, it reminded him that Trev was meant to call him back. He reached into his phone and thumbed the screen to bring it to life. "Ah, fuck." He could afford to not pay attention to the cops. With his team and Commander Hurt surrounding them, there was little which could happen without causing a ruckus.

"What's wrong?" Becky leaned into his side.

"My phone has been on a call to my ma all along."

"Your mom is on the phone?"

"Yes, dearie, his mom is on the phone." A woman's voice came from the phone. "I can't hear what's going on. Someone needs to put me on speaker phone."

"Oh. My. God."

It wasn't only Becky's face which was going red. He could

feel the heat climbing up the back of his neck. He put the phone to his ear. "Sorry, Ma, I'll call you back later." He pressed end on the call, and it immediately rang again.

"Is that your mom again?"

He glanced at the phone again. "Not unless my mother suddenly learned how to block her number." He owed Trev big time for being faster on the redial than his mother was. "It's Trev." He answered the call. "Hey, bro."

"What the fuck happened?" Trev growled. "You call me out of bed then are on the phone for fucking hours? I was just about to call Draven."

"Sorry about that, I butt dialed my ma."

"What?"

Yeah, he'd probably have that sound of disbelief in his voice if he was their comms dude, too. He squeezed his eyes shut and blew out a slow breath. "We're at the police station. Mozart's been arrested."

"Cops in San D. are still fucking batshit," Trev muttered. "Let me make a call. If that doesn't work, Riga is on his way." There was some background noise which Kentucky couldn't make out. "The boss left twenty minutes ago, and he's pissed."

"I'll bet." Yeah, he'd be pissed if he had to leave his wife just when she was about to pop out a longed-for baby, too. If Nemesis decided he deserved a punch, he'd take it on the chin gladly.

"Jeep went with him."

"Fabulous." If Jeep's wife had sent him down here to take over Becky's protection, then shit was gonna fly, and his friend had better remember how he'd backed him all the way across the damn compound where they'd rescued their women from. If he didn't, then Kentucky wouldn't be long about telling him to back the hell off. "Is it still Chief Dunn in charge down there?"

"Yeah."

"Gimme a minute." The phone went dead and Kentucky shoved it back into his pocket.

Somewhere in the background of the police station, another phone rang, and a man's voice called the chief of police.

"Do not leave," Chief Dunn ordered.

"We aren't going anywhere until this matter is resolved," Commander Hurt replied. "You have my word."

"What's happening?" Becky asked.

"I'm not sure, doll." He led her to a row of seats. "Why don't you sit down for a bit?"

"I'm taller standing."

The snark was so out of the left field, he barked out a laugh. "Yeah, you sure are." He'd never been more grateful that she'd been wearing yoga pants and a t-shirt when she'd come down to the kitchen. He'd have lost his mind if she'd had to come here in her jammies. Because asking her to change her clothes would have been totally out of the question. It would have meant leaving her out of his sight. That wasn't happening. "But sit down anyway, because we're gonna be here a while, I think."

"I was afraid of that." She pressed her fingers into the back of her neck and pushed back against them as if there was a knot there and she was trying to find relief. "Why are they being obtuse?"

"Covering their bases, I think." He sat down and tugged her to sit next to him. "May I?" He covered the fingers on her neck with his hand. "Tell me now if you'd prefer to do it yourself."

"Please." She pulled her hand out from under his. "I can't quite reach the spot. It aches."

Kentucky pressed with his fingers. He decided if she was

going to ignore the fact all the guys were surrounding them, then he'd follow her lead. "Here?"

"Hmm, a little further to the middle."

No wonder she was so stressed, her neck and shoulders were so freaking tight, they had to hurt. He pushed and probed with his fingers, using the quiet sounds she gave him to guide his placement and how hard he pressed against her. When she stiffened and then relaxed, he knew he had the right place. "I got you." Maybe if he repeated it enough, she'd believe him.

"What's happening?"

He followed her gaze to where the chief of police was talking to Mozart, Benny, and Commander Hurt. Mozart was released from his cuffs, and he rubbed at his wrists. "I don't know." Kentucky gathered her hair in one hand and placed it over one shoulder. "It looks like they are letting him go."

"I don't understand."

"Me either." He warily watched Commander Hurt rub the spot between his eyebrows as if he had a headache.

I know the feeling, bro.

Kentucky was more than sure he had done the same thing more than once in the last few hours. He watched as the man who'd once been his commanding officer crossed the precinct floor toward him and Becky.

"We're outta here." Commander Hurt's voice was calm as ever, but the clenched fists at his sides told their own story. The man was pissed as all get out. "Let's go, Smith, Ma'am."

"Yes, sir ." Kentucky got to his feet. "Where to?"

"Follow me."

"Roger that."

CHAPTER SIX

Becky wasn't entirely sure what was happening. But from how Kentucky urged her to her feet and hustled her out of the police station and back to the car, she was guessing it had to be a good thing. "Is Mozart okay? Is he still in trouble?"

"I don't think so."

"It's just weird how they seem to have just changed his mind."

"Bet ya ten bucks Trev had something to do with it," Caleb said from the front seat. He turned over the engine. "It wouldn't be the first time he found a way for us to get out of a tricky spot."

"You've all been hauled into a police station for questioning before?" While she'd spent some time in Montana with these people, most of it had been spent in either the medical facility or with Lina and Willow.

And Kentucky.

She didn't need reminding. Yes, she'd spent some time with Kentucky, too. Okay, more than a little. But that was neither here nor there right now.

"Not in this country." Kentucky answered her question

when the two men in the front seats clammed up at her question.

"But you have in other countries?" Did they make a habit of doing this kind of thing? She wasn't sure how she felt about that.

"Yes." Kentucky lifted one shoulder. "But I can't tell you about it without clearance from Dalton."

Dalton is Lina's husband.

"Okay."

"That's it?" he asked. "Just okay?"

"If you say you can't talk about it, then why would I keep bugging you about it?" She narrowed her eyes at him. "Will your answer change if I do?"

"Well, no, no it won't."

"Then it's a waste of our time for me to do it."

"Dude, you are one lucky bastard." Draven half turned in his seat and winked at her. "How the hell did you get lucky enough to find a woman who doesn't keep asking the same question multiple times until she drives you nuts?"

"No idea," Kentucky replied. "I'm keeping her, so keep your paws to yourself, Kilkenny, or I'll make you regret it."

She loved how these men did their best to not cross some imaginary line and upset her. She had no idea what that line was—*wait—what did he say?*

She turned the conversation over in her mind. 'I'm keeping her.' What on earth did that mean? It couldn't possibly mean what she thought it did... right?

"Don't think about it too hard," Kentucky whispered close to her. "There is no hidden meaning in my words."

Hello, girly bits. I did not invite you to this party. I'm still trying to wrap my head around what he means.

She refused to give any indication of the inner turmoil she felt and managed a small smile before turning to look out the window. The flash of a signpost made her brain stumble to a stop. The panic she'd been fighting all night came roaring back to life and welled up inside her. "Where—where are we going? Where are you taking me?"

"Pull over, right now," Kentucky demanded.

"Yes, sir." Caleb flashed the vehicle in front of them and immediately whipped the truck onto the hard shoulder.

"Get out, boys." Kentucky pointed to the door on Draven's side. "Give us a minute."

"No, no. It's fine."

"No, it's not." As soon as the doors slammed behind Caleb and Draven, Kentucky turned to her. "Tell me where you are at, doll?" He raised his hand to her face and gently cupped her cheek, refusing to let her look at her hands. "Before we move another inch, I need to know you are okay."

She swallowed past the lump in her throat. It was probably ridiculously stupid to have gotten in the truck if she didn't want to be taken where he was bringing her. But in her defense, he'd lulled her into some kind of trance as he'd massaged her neck. "Where are we going?"

"Based on the direction we're headed," he pointed to another sign on the side of the road, "we're going to Riverton. Rexar's family is there. He, his wife, and their son are staying with friends."

Oh, god. More strangers.

She breathed slowly as she absorbed the information. If Rexar's family was there, then it meant it was somewhere safe, right? He didn't strike her as a man who'd put the ones he loved in danger. "Who are the friends?"

"Matthew Steel and his wife Caroline." Kentucky thankfully didn't pressure her or push her. Here on the side of the highway, he gave her the information she asked for. "Wolf works with Mozart and Benny. It's a safe place for us in this part of the world."

"Okay."

"Doll." He ran his thumb across her cheek. "If you want me to find us a hotel instead, you just say the word and I'll go talk to Commander Hurt and make it happen."

"No, just give me a minute."

"Take all the time you need."

He was being way too kind. They were on the hard shoulder. Not the safest place on the planet to be, especially not with all the eighteen wheelers speeding by making the truck shake in their wake. But she appreciated it more than he would ever know.

She wasn't trying to be difficult. But as much as she craved the protection being near him offered, there was no way she was going to allow him or his teammates to walk all over her and bully her into hiding.

If that's too stupid to live, then they're just going to have to deal, because the last time I went for a drive with someone, I ended up in a freaking container. Kentucky is not like them.

She knew he wasn't. Deep inside, she knew none of these men were like the ones who had taken her. "I can leave if I want to?"

"Yes," Kentucky promised. "If you want to leave or you aren't comfortable, I'll find somewhere that works better for you."

Okay. I can do this. I trust him.

Trusting someone she shouldn't have was what got her into the mess Kentucky had rescued her and Willow from. If he dropped her into a similar mess, she was going to be so fricking mad. Sit on her couch with wine in her pajamas mad. But somehow, she knew he wouldn't do that to her. He'd die first. She nodded. "Okay. I'm good now. I'm sorry I made you all stop."

"No, doll." He leaned down until his lips hovered over hers. "I want you to tell me when you need to me slow down.

I may not always think it's too fast. But when I mess up, I need you to promise to tell me."

She dropped her gaze from his eyes to his lips and immediately made herself look back into his eyes to search for the truth there. "Okay."

"Good." He pressed a soft, swift kiss to her lips. "Remember, you tell me when to slow down and I do," he told her. "I promise I'll slow down if you say so."

"I know." She believed him. Was she an idiot for doing so? Maybe. But she needed to know she could trust not only him, but herself, too. "I'm ready."

"Okay. Then let's get back on the road." He hit the button for the window and pushed one hand out, clearly in some kind of signal, as Caleb and Draven got back into the truck.

"Everything good?" Draven reached for his seat belt. "Are we going back?"

"No. We're going to your friends' place." Somehow, she knew she had to be the one to reply, or they'd be headed straight back to San Diego.

"Are you sure?" Caleb flipped on the flicker and glanced at her over his shoulder.

She nudged Kentucky with her elbow when he growled under his breath. She appreciated that his people were being so considerate, and if he pulled out that notebook of his, she was going to snatch it from his hands and toss it out the window. "I promise, I'm sure," she reassured the men in the front. "If that changes, you'll be the second to know."

"Who's the first?"

"The growly bear next to me."

"Hah, she has your number, Ken." Caleb pulled them back out into traffic after the truck in front of them.

"Yeah, she does."

I wonder why he doesn't sound one bit displeased about that.

She'd have plenty of time to think about it between here

and where they were going. She covered her mouth with her hand and yawned behind it.

"Sleep for a while." Kentucky placed his arm over the back of the seat. "Snuggle in. I promise I'll wake you when we get to Riverton."

"Hmm."

CHAPTER SEVEN

He couldn't remember a time where he hadn't been the one driving the truck. As Bravo Team's commander, he typically led from the front. But as Becky slept against his shoulder, he couldn't bring himself to care. He gently brushed his fingers over the top of her shoulder and she snuggled in close. Yup. Kentucky didn't care about ridiculous things like sitting in the back seats anymore.

"Boss?" Draven didn't turn his head as he spoke softly.

"Yes?"

"It's almost two in the morning. Are we seriously turning up at Steel's house without letting him know?" Draven asked. "Because that would be asking for trouble if it happened at the ranch."

"Yeah, I would normally agree." He rubbed the ends of her hair between his thumb and index finger. His need and desire to be connected to her hadn't abated since she'd moved down here to San Diego like he'd thought it would. If anything, it had gotten stronger. "But we're just following the boys in front. If Commander Hurt tells us to follow him, what else are we supposed to do?"

"True."

"Don't matter." Caleb flipped on his flicker and took the exit off the highway. "Because I think we're almost there anyway."

He glanced out the window. "Yeah." Leaning his head down to Becky's, he whispered softly in her ear. "Hey, doll, we are almost there." As much as he hated to wake her up, he'd promised he would before they arrived. Kentucky figured he knew her well enough at this point to not want her to wake up in a strange place with more strangers around her.

"Mmh." She sighed softly and burrowed into his chest.

"Becky?" He ran his hand up and down her arm. "We're gonna be pulling into the house in a minute. You need to wake up, okay?"

"No. Stay sleeping. Safe here."

Her sleepy words stabbed him right in the soul. She trusted him. Somewhere deep down, he'd known that, but hearing her say she wanted to stay sleeping in his arms… man, that made him want things he had no business wanting whatsoever. Yet here he was with his heart doing some kind of weird little flip-flop shit.

I'm probably a fucking idiot for wanting more. But I do, no matter how much I know my heart is going to be ripped out of my damn chest.

Caleb parallel parked on the street outside Matthew Steel's house. The driveway was full already by Steel's wife's car, his truck, and Commander Hurt's truck. Time was up, they were here, and she needed to wake up.

"We'll, uh, see you inside." Draven got out of the truck and slammed the door after him, making her jump and jerk awake. Becky pressed herself against the door, one hand behind her as if she was searching for the door handle. Just as soon as his hands were free, he was adding that shit in his notebook.

"Hey, it's me. It's Kentucky." He kept his voice even and soothing. "I swear you are okay."

"I—" Caleb shut up and got out of the truck when she yelped at the sound of his voice. They'd all had nightmares or had woken out of a deep sleep at one point or other. They all understood that sometimes it took your brain a minute to catch up and overtake your panic.

"Becky? Doll, I swear it's just me. The other two are going in the house. You're safe. I swear it." He could just about make out her face under the light which filtered into the truck from the streetlights. The fear in her eyes… if those bastards weren't dead already, he'd have been right back there on that construction site looking for more assholes to rip apart limb from limb. "You are safe, doll, I got you."

As if those three little words, *I got you*, were the ones which broke through the fear, she lifted her gaze to his. "Tuck?"

"Yes, baby, Tuck." He fucking loved that she called him that. Very few people ever had. It had been the name his father called him, and he'd made it a habit to either ignore anyone else who tried to use it or had to swallow down the hurt which still filled his heart even after all these years, if it was during a mission and one of the guys used the name.

"Did I screw up?"

"Hell no." Fucking unbelievable. She was the one who was traumatized and here she was, worrying if she'd upset other people. Man, she was something else. "You didn't screw up, I swear."

"It feels like I did."

"I know." He reached out and tucked her hair behind her ear. She didn't flinch away from him. He was taking that as a win. "But you didn't. Even if you had, only me and the guys were in the truck. They'd never say a word about it." He could tell she didn't quite believe him when she lowered her eyelids and looked down. "Hey." He slowly slid across the seat until he was next to her. "I promise you, neither of them thinks you did anything wrong. If they did, they are the type to tell you straight out."

"Okay."

He wasn't sure if he should ask for what he needed or wanted to. But he couldn't resist. He had a feeling they were going to be surrounded by people for the next while and there would be little opportunity for time just spent with Becky. "Can I have a hug before we go in there?"

She hesitated for a split second, then turned into him, laying her head over his heart and one arm around his waist. "I'd like that."

He smiled against her hair and wrapped around her, carefully at first, in case she wasn't quite as ready as she thought. Once he felt the fingers on the hand around his waist bunch into his shirt, he tightened his hold. He could almost hear the wheels in her brain spinning and decided he'd just wait and see what she needed or wanted to say. She'd been pushed past her limits more than once tonight. She didn't need him adding to the mix.

"I didn't think I'd ever be able to hug someone again." Her voice was so low he had to bend his head almost down to her lips to hear them. "I'm happy I can hug you, Tuck."

"Me, too, baby doll, me, too." Now that he'd combined the two names he'd been using for her together, he realized how much they fit her.

Baby doll, that's my Becky.

"I think I'm ready now."

She might be, but he wasn't. "Okay." He pressed a kiss to the top of her head. "Stay here and I'll come around and get the door."

"I can—"

He pressed his finger to her lips. "I know you can, baby doll, but I like opening doors for you, okay?" He smiled at her when she nodded in reply. "Thank you." Kentucky finally released Becky and scooted across the seat to the other side. He took the opportunity to adjust the tightness of his pants as he rounded the back of the truck. He opened the door and held out his hand to her. "Ma'am."

She snorted out a laugh at how he'd attempted to sound like those British butlers on one of the TV shows the women at the ranch liked and placed her fingers in his palm. "Why thank you, kind sir."

Kentucky swapped her fingers to his other hand and placed his now free one on her lower back, guiding her toward the door. "Lean on me if you need to in there," he told her softly. "But I promise these are good people."

"Okay."

That had to be good enough for now. He glanced over his shoulder to make sure he'd shut the truck before he knocked softly on the front door.

CHAPTER EIGHT

Breathe. Breathe. Breathe. Keep breathing. A purple face from lack of oxygen is so not the first impression you give the people you've never met before.

Becky was fairly sure her mental reminder was the only thing reminding her lungs what they were meant to do. Thankfully, Kentucky kept the hand on her back in place or she'd have been tempted to turn right around and disappear into the streets, just so she could find a bolt hole to hide in.

"Hey, Kentucky." A tall man with dark hair answered the door. He smiled at her. "Hi." Thankfully, he didn't reach for her or even look like he was about to. Instead, he just opened the door wider to allow them to come in. "I'm Matt, or Wolf, if you prefer."

"Hi." She'd never thought she'd sounded shy in her life. But right now she absolutely sounded shy or reserved or something.

"Wolf, this is my Becky."

She glanced at Kentucky out of the corner of her eye. Was she imagining the slight infliction on the word 'my.' No, she didn't think she was. She also could admit to herself that she kind of liked it. Wasn't she the idiot?

"Hi, Becky." Wolf turned and walked deeper into the house. "Come meet my wife, Caroline."

He has a wife. She'll keep him in line.

"Hey, Ice." Wolf wrapped his arms around the only woman in the room. "Meet Becky... Kentucky's woman."

Kentucky's woman?

Is he crazy?

There is no way I am ever going to be good enough to be anyone's woman again. Never mind Kentucky's.

"Can I make you some tea?" Caroline's smile welcomed her into her home. "We have a child sleeping in the basement. So, we need to be quiet. But we can make tea, and if you are hungry, I have leftovers in the fridge." As she spoke, she bustled around the kitchen, filling a kettle and putting it on the stove.

"I'll get out of your way." Wolf tugged on the ends of Caroline's hair, his hand wrapped around her neck, and he placed a kiss on her forehead. "I'll be out back with the guys if you want to join us when your tea is ready."

"Love you." Caroline petted his cheek and smiled back at him. "Kentucky, do you want tea or coffee?"

"Coffee, if you have it, please. Thank you, Ma'am."

"Didn't we have a conversation about you all calling me Ma'am?" Caroline leaned out of the cupboard she'd been taking mugs out of and quirked up her eyebrow at him.

"You did, but my ma drummed manners into me, then the Navy reenforced it." He smiled at her. "So, the chances of it changing in the next few days are about slim to none, I think."

It's all so freaking normal.

Becky watched the interactions between Wolf and Caroline, and also between Kentucky and Caroline. It settled the disquiet inside her. She'd been worried she'd feel out of place here, with these people. But somehow, while she was still nervous, feeling out of place didn't seem to be on the agenda tonight. "I'm sorry you had to stay up so late for us to get here." She had to apologize. These people were going out of their way to help them—help her. She appreciated it more than she'd ever be able to express.

"I don't mind at all." Caroline filled a mug of coffee from the pot next to the stove and handed it to Kentucky. "I love when my house is full of people. It feels more homey." She pointed to the door. "Shoo, Kentucky, go find the men." She glanced at Becky as soon as she'd said it. "Unless you'd prefer that he stay?"

Damn, Caroline was astute, or maybe it had been her sharp inhale of breath which had let the other woman know she wasn't totally comfortable. Becky coughed and cleared her throat. She managed a smile for them both. "It's okay, Tuck. I'll be okay here."

He looked skeptical of her reassurance, but nodded and gave her a smile, which warmed her down to her toes. "I'm right through that room there." He pointed to the living room. "Just go through the French doors and I'm right there."

"Okay." What else could she say without being rude? She watched him leave, but stayed in the kitchen.

"I'm sorry if I overstepped." Caroline pulled out a wooden box and placed it on the counter. "We can go sit with the guys if it's easier on you."

"No, no. It's okay, I don't mind." She couldn't just stay standing here in the middle of the kitchen like an idiot. She made her feet take first one step and then another until she was next to Caroline at the counter. She ran her fingertip over the beautifully carved lid of the box. "It's so pretty."

"Isn't it?" Caroline moved to the other side of the stove, giving her space. "My friend Tex sent it to me." Her entire face lit up when she mentioned his name. Almost like when Wolf had kissed her, but not quite. "Open it up and pick which tea you'd like."

"You have really lovely friends." She flipped up the lid and even she knew her eyes had widened. "Wow."

"Yeah, Tex kinda went overboard, didn't he?"

That was an understatement. The box was stuffed to the brim with every flavor of tea on the planet. "I don't know how I can choose."

"Maybe some chamomile," Caroline suggested. "It might help you sleep."

Becky folded her lips together to prevent screaming 'no.' Her stomach churned, revolting at the thoughts of the tea, which had been the catalyst for tonight's shit show. Even though it hadn't been the tea at fault, she would forever associate chamomile tea with seeing those shackles in her kitchen. "No—no chamomile."

Oh, no. I screwed up.

"I know that look," Caroline said softly. "You didn't screw up."

"Are you reading my mind?" She moved to one side as Caroline reached for the tea box.

Caroline flipped through the tiny, colorful packets. "No, not at all. My friend Fiona sometimes gets a similar look on her face. She's Cookie's woman." She picked a pink packet and nudged the box back toward Becky. "She might tell you the reason why some time. But let's just say there are times I wish most men could be neutered like dogs."

"Yeah." Holy cowbells, it sounded like Fiona knew or at least understood how she had no control over where her brain decided to take her. "I'd like that sometime, if she's okay with it."

"I'll call her in the morning, she'll be over with Alabama, who's with Abe." Caroline promised. She took the now boiling kettle off the stove and poured the water into one mug. "Did you pick a tea?"

"Um." Her fingers fumbled over the packets and she picked up one. "Yes, blackberry and vanilla."

"Oh, that's a yummy one." Caroline waited for her to drop the bag in the mug and then filled it with boiling water for her. "Can you grab a bottle of water from the bottom shelf of the fridge, please? If I try to drink this straight away, I'll burn the mouth off myself, and Wolf will be cross about it." Caroline grinned at her. "He seems to like my mouth in working order, even if that working order is telling him to put his boots away."

"Of course." Having something to do made all the awkwardness of meeting new people a lot easier. She was guessing Caroline knew that, though. When she turned around with the water in her hand, Caroline was up on the counter, reaching into the top shelf of one of the cupboards. "Are you meant to be up there like that?"

"No, don't tell my husband." Caroline's voice was muffled. "Even though he's the one who put the good cookies on the top shelf and totally forgot, I'm about half his height."

"My lips are sealed."

"I knew I liked you." Caroline shuffled along the counter and held out a metal tin. "Can you grab this for me?"

There was no way she wanted Caroline to fall and hurt herself. She had a feeling that wouldn't go over well with any of the men. She reached up and grabbed the box. "I got it."

"Thanks." Caroline jumped to the floor, swung the cupboard door closed, and grinned at her. "Short girl problems."

"You aren't exactly short, though."

"Compared to the boys, I am."

"I think anyone but a gorilla would be shorter than all of

them." She followed Caroline to the table, carrying both their mugs.

"Truth." Caroline popped the lid off the tin and held it out to her. "Chocolate hobnobs. I don't know who sent them to us." She smiled. "But when I make Matthew tell me, I swear I'm going to beg them for more."

Becky pulled a cookie from the packet and studied it. "I don't know what a hobnob is."

"It's oaty, chocolatey goodness, which spends a minute on your lips and before you know it, you've eaten a whole package."

She nibbled on the edge of her cookie, flavor exploding over her tongue. "Oh, wow, these are insanely good."

"Told you so." Caroline grinned at her over the rim of her mug. "Apparently, if you make English tea, they are awesome if you dip them in it before eating them. But I haven't tried that way yet, as I'm afraid it will crumble off in my tea."

"Yeah, I'm not sure I'd like lumpy tea either." She blew over the rim of her mug and cautiously sipped her tea.

"Why do you look surprised?" Caroline asked.

Crap. She needed to remaster putting the blank look back on her face. "I don't normally like blackberries," she admitted. "But this is so good." She knew she'd been taking a risk with blackberry tea, but hadn't wanted to seem picky when she'd realized which one she'd picked.

"Why didn't you say something?" Caroline cocked her head to one side. "You could have just picked another one."

"I know." She lifted one shoulder and rubbed it off her ear. "But I promise I like this tea. I'd tell you if I didn't." And just like that, she knew it was true. There was something about this house, this woman, these people which, as ridiculous as it sounded, even in her own head, made her feel like she belonged.

CHAPTER NINE

John *Tex* Keegan rubbed his knee. As much as he didn't like to remove his prosthetic leg, doing so after a long day was such a relief. "It's not as if I ran forty freaking klicks. It shouldn't be this damn sore." He rubbed the salve on the sore spots. This one had arrived from Dalton Knight via Fedex this morning, as a thank you for helping Rexar find Lily and RJ. As much as he appreciated the gesture, he wrinkled his nose and squinted his eyes against the burn. "Man, that stinks. I swear if there is horse piss or something in there, I'm going to divert Knight's damn plane to freaking Siberia or something."

He glanced at his computer screen as if he expected it to answer him. He knew it wouldn't. Computers only sang or answered you when they were commanded to do so by a set of fingers on the keyboard.

"Keep telling yourself that you're watching the screen for intel." He screwed the top on the salve jar and pushed it to the back of the desk. "But in reality, you know you are waiting for *her* to pop up in your inbox." He smiled around the rim of his glass when he thought of her. She was hitting him right in the feels and she didn't even know it. If it turned out she was sent to cause trouble or to get into his systems, he was going to be so mad with himself for allowing himself the indulgence of having her to talk to. His computer pinged.

CC_CopyCat: Hey, you. I just wanted to check in and see if you got things fixed for your friend.

His day was already better, and he smiled at the screen before typing back a response.

Tex: Yeah, everything is fixed now, and all is quiet on the Western Front.

CC_CopyCat: Don't jinx it. Touch wood or something.

What did she just say?

Tex: ...?

CC_CopyCat: When you don't want to jinx something, and you might have, you find a wooden object and tap it. Have you not heard that before?

Tex: No. I thought you mean—

He hit backspace. There was no way on the planet he was telling her he thought she was telling him to touch his dick. That was way over the line of where their friendship was at this point. Instead, he left what he had been about to say at just one word.

Tex: No.

He could see the little dots on the corner of the message box flickering as if she was writing a message. It stopped and started about three times before her message finally came in.

CC_CopyCat: Did I overstep some line I can't see?

Tex: No, I promise. I misread what you said is all. I must be tired. It's been a long few days.

CC_CopyCat: I'll let you get some rest.

"Damn it, that's not what I meant at all."

Tex: No, CC, talking to you is the highlight of my day. Please don't go just yet.

He had barely hit send when his phone buzzed on the

desk next to him. He knew without even looking at it this was the end of his free evening. Tex thumbed the screen and opened the message.

CC_CopyCat: Okay, are we going to play? Kick some monster butt?

If only she knew the real-life monsters whose asses he helped kick from behind his computers on what felt like a daily basis at this point. Would she run, or would she be intrigued?

Tex: Hang on… phone.

CC_CopyCat: Take your time.

Wolf: Call me. Stat.

Crap, what happened? He scooted his chair a little to the right to his work computer and moved the mouse to light up the screen. Once he'd tapped in his password, he pulled up the secure app they used for phone calls and typed in Wolf's number from memory.

"Hey, Tex. Thanks for calling me back."

"What's going on, bro?"

"Can you look up a situation for me?" Wolf asked. "Not a work one, but something Nemesis was involved with a few months back."

"Sure. Gimme the details."

"Remember Eli Black?"

"Of course, I do." Hell yes, Tex remembered Eli Black. He'd been there when he'd died. The same incident had been why Tex was no longer a SEAL. "What shit was he in?"

"Not Eli," Wolf said. "His daughter Willow."

"Fuck."

"Yeah," Wolf continued. "A few months back she was kidnapped, and Jeep Ford lost his shit and shredded a construction site outside of Billings to get her back. He married her a couple of weeks later."

"Jeep Ford married Willow Black?" Crap, was that the

wedding invitation which had come in the post? The one sitting still unopened on his kitchen table with the stack of other invites which had come over the years? "What did Nemesis say?"

"Apparently there was a dust up, but you know those two. They sorted it."

"Yeah. I'll bet it wasn't fun being around them for a while though."

"Truth." Wolf snickered. "But I do have a reason for calling you, and not because you didn't go to the wedding."

"Hit me." He pulled his other keyboard toward him and tapped out a message.

Tex: I gotta run for a bit. I'll ping you when I get done.

CC_CopyCat: Ok. Be safe.

Tex: I promise I'm not leaving my desk. Safe is in my wheelhouse.

CC_CopyCat: A pen may bite you.

"Yo, Tex, you still there?"

"Sorry, I was just finishing up something." Crap, how often did he have trouble multi-tasking? Count this as a first.

"When Nemesis rescued Willow Black, they also rescued Becky Jones."

"You have a date of birth?"

"It's not her I need to know about," Wolf said. "Well, it sort of is."

Tex could hear the frustration in his friend's voice. Wolf Steel was all about protecting the innocent.

"Nemesis organized for her to rent out Mozart's place in San Diego."

"Good thinking," Tex replied, then tagged on, "never tell Nemesis I said that."

"I won't. His head is big enough," Wolf agreed. "Earlier tonight, Kentucky Smith went down there to visit her and walked in on a situation."

"Let me guess, she was in trouble?" He pulled a notebook close to him and flipped through the pages until he found the one he wanted. It took two seconds to pull up a search engine and type in the address Wolf's team used for their security systems, going in a back door to the cameras.

"Shackles placed on the counter behind her while she was making tea, trouble."

"Shit." He freaking hated when assholes preyed on women. "I'm just pulling up the feed now. It will only take a second." It might be Wolf calling him to tell him what happened. But when his resources were needed to fix something or find information, he preferred to see the incident firsthand if he could.

"No worries," Wolf replied. "Mozart figured you'd have tabs on the property."

"Ha, it's as if he knows me." He frowned at the screen. "Two of the cameras are out. Tell Mozart to fix them."

"Yup."

He double clicked on the other camera, this one from the front of the property, and hit play, then fast forwarded until he saw movement. "Unmarked cops were in front of the property?"

"So Kentucky says." Wolf explained what Tex was looking at on the screen. "He rolled up just as they were changing shifts."

Tex flipped screens and got to work, letting himself into the NCIC (National Crime Information Center) looking for information on why those cops were at Mozart's house. "I got a report Becky Jones went in three days ago to report a stalker." He frowned at the screen as the doors of the cop cars flew open and the officers raced across the street to the front door. "I'm guessing the black truck fishtailing into the drive is our boy Smith?" He didn't need Wolf to answer, as he could see Kentucky racing for the house with some others on his heels. "Who's with him?"

"Most of Bravo Team."

"Figures." Tex continued to watch everything play out. "What am I looking for?"

"Kentucky wants to know if anyone survived the raid in Montana," Wolf replied. "Because someone somewhere knows Becky was there."

"Yeah, that makes the most sense." Tex scribbled some notes. "I'll get with Nemesis's tech guys and get all that intel, then see if I can track a survivor."

"Tell him to look at an ATF agent, too."

"That you, Smith?"

"Yeah." Kentucky's voice was slightly distant, as if he was further way from the phone than Wolf was. "The ATF dude was the only guy breathing when we left there with the girls."

"This intel right here is why we use secure networks to call about work shit," Tex muttered. "All y'all would be incriminating yourselves with the brass and fuck knows who else if we didn't."

"The brass is here, too," another voice chimed in.

His eyes widened, because holy cow, he recognized that voice. Hell, he spoke to that voice at least twice a mission when needed. "Hey, Commander, what's doing?"

"Hah."

Tex didn't think Commander Hurt would have an issue with him figuring out why Kentucky's woman was being targeted. After all, the woman he was seeing had once been trafficked and rescued with Cookie's woman Fiona. "I'm not going anything illegal." He was throwing that out there.

"Much." The humor in Commander Hurt's voice was more than clear. "You forgot to add 'much' to the end of that sentence."

He barked out a laugh. "Must be the TBI. Makes my memory shit sometimes."

"Sure, sure," Commander Hurt said. "See you remember that, if you get caught."

"You think so little of me?" Tex snarked back. He missed working with these men. They had been his team, his chosen brothers, for a long time. "Let me dig and see what I can find," he told them. "I'll be back to you in a bit."

"No worries," Wolf replied and hung up.

Tex took a second to message CC_CopyCat and let her know his evening was shot to hell and gaming was no longer in his plan. Then he got to work. Finding the person terrorizing Kentucky's woman would be a freaking pleasure.

CHAPTER TEN

"I'm so fucking happy he's on our side." Kentucky had no qualms about saying it. There wasn't a man in this garden who would consider John Keegan a threat to national security.

"Damn straight." Commander Hurt drained his coffee and placed the mug on the table. "What's the plan to keep your lady safe?"

"I'll take her back to Montana with me."

"And if she won't go?" Mozart ran his hand across his face, scratching at the top of the scar which marred his cheek. "There's a reason she was renting my house, remember?"

"I know." He'd have to figure out a way to make it happen. Behind the Texas gates of Nemesis Ranch, she'd be safe. But even as he considered it, he could hear her words from before she'd moved down here to California. 'A prison made of gold is still a prison, Tuck. I have spent enough time locked away in the dark. I need to be free.' "Damn it."

"What are you all complaining about?" Caroline's voice

drew their attention. She led Becky out of the house. When Wolf held out one arm, Caroline sat in his lap.

Kentucky smiled up at Becky and shifted over on the swing seat he'd been using. He didn't make the big gesture with his arm as Wolf had, but instead he nodded to the space he'd freed up and thankfully she took it, but perched on the edge of the seat. Kentucky braced his feet on the ground to make sure it didn't move and tip her off onto the patio. "Settle in, Doll Face. I got you."

"Okay," Becky whispered and shuffled back until her feet were off the ground. "Thank you."

"You're welcome." He dropped one arm over the back of the seat and she snuggled in against him. He didn't even think she was aware she was doing it, but he wouldn't change it for a second.

"Do I want to know what's happening?" Caroline asked.

"We're trying to figure out what happens next." Rexar picked up his mug. "And if Miss Becky comes back with us to Montana or if we have to find somewhere else to keep her safe?"

Kentucky felt her stiffen against him, but when she started to pull away, he touched her shoulder with his fingers. "This isn't a slight, and it doesn't mean you are a bother. So forget that thought ever entered your head right now."

"How did you know that's—"

"Because I know how your beautiful brain works." How could she not see it? Everything about her fascinated him. She was the flame, and he was the moth who couldn't stay away. He refused to believe he was going to get burned. Unless it from their bed as it went up in flames from the heat which flared between them. "You are not causing problems, and you aren't a bother."

"You've thought of everything."

She was freaking adorable. She wasn't quite going toe-to-toe with him, but she was making sure her voice didn't get lost. "I'm so proud of you." He whispered the words softly. "Don't let anyone walk all over you, even me."

"That will never happen again."

"Good." He smiled at her, then nodded to the people around them. "But we do need to figure out where we go next."

"I can make room on the couch—"

"Thank you, Caroline, but you have Rexar, Lily, and their son staying here." Kentucky didn't want to sound like an asshole. He was grateful for all the help. But he also wanted Becky to have some space, if that was what she needed.

"I can go crash with Mozart," Benny said. "You can have my place."

Kentucky opened his mouth and snapped it shut again when Becky elbowed him.

"I think maybe I should leave town," Becky said slowly. "I don't want to bring trouble to your doors. You all have families." She dug her elbow into his side once again when he drew in a breath. "I will not put more people in danger."

"There might be a place," Mozart said slowly. "In the mountains, if that's your thing?"

"Mountains?" Becky cocked her head to one side. "I could do mountains."

"It's up by Big Bear Lake," Mozart said. "I was planning on going up there to hike some weekend, but haven't gotten around to it yet." He lifted one shoulder. "It might be a decent place to regroup. It's close enough that we can get to you if you need backup, and it should have enough space that you aren't tripping over people while you figure out your next move."

Sign me up. I like the sound of that.

But it wasn't his decision to make. As much as he wanted

to be the one deciding, Becky had to agree. "What do you think?"

"Um." She chewed on the corner of her lip. "I think it wouldn't hurt to have a few days to see if we can figure out what's going on. And it's close enough to get back if we need to go back to the police station."

Damn, I forgot about that.

"Mozart, how come you aren't still in the slammer?"

"I'm not sure." Mozart looked to Commander Hurt. "Did you have something to do with it?" When the commander shook his head, Mozart added on, "Or Jag?"

"I didn't call Jag," Commander Hurt said. "The only person anyone spoke to was Nemesis HQ."

"Freaking Trev." Rexar scratched the scruff on his face. "That asshole has more tentacles than an octopus."

He might have, but Kentucky was grateful Mozart wasn't sharing a cell with Bubba and keeping his ass to the wall tonight while they waited for Jag to do their thing. "Do you think he and Tex exchange tips on how to get our butts out of trouble?"

"Probably," Caleb chimed in. "I'm betting there is a knitting circle with all the tech dudes and they exchange recipes for new shit all the time."

"Patterns, not recipes."

"Huh, pardon, Miss Becky?" A look of confusion crossed Caleb's face.

"Knitting circles have patterns, not recipes," Becky told him. "At least any of the ones I went to have."

"You knit?"

"Badly." She grinned at him. "But I figured if I knew how to wield a knitting needle, then it was almost as good as carrying a weapon when, or rather, if I answer the door."

"That's an awesome idea." Caroline leaned around Wolf's

arm. "I'm going to order a set on Amazon and put them in the letter holder next to the door, just in case."

"Ice..."

"Shh. You go to work sometimes," Caroline reminded Wolf. "You all do. It's not premeditated if I stab someone with a knitting needle I just happened to have lying around."

"I like the way you think." Becky leaned forward and high-fived Caroline.

Damn, look at his girl, finding her groove. He and Wolf exchanged glances over the girls' heads and gave each other a chin lift in acknowledgement. "Nem is still on the way, right?"

"Shit." Rexar winced. "No, Lina went into labor and I told him to divert his ass back home. Nobody should miss the birth of their child." Rexar had not only missed his own son's birth but also the first years of his life, thanks to a double-crossing a-hole and way too long spent in an Iranian prison.

Kentucky totally understood why they'd told Dalton to go back. Thankfully, their boss wasn't locked up in some shit-hole prison in Iran. "You did good," he reassured Rexar. "I would have told him to go home, too."

"You all should go home," Becky said. "I can go to the place Mozart said..."

"No." He wasn't even going to entertain that idea for a second, and definitely not for a full minute. "I stay with you until we figure out what's happening and how to fix it."

CHAPTER ELEVEN

"Bossy much?" It was so frustrating that she wasn't able to do this by herself. How much longer before she found her feet again? She could manage an entire class of toddlers at one point. Now she couldn't even make a decision because reality had slapped her in the face one time too many.

"Baby, I'm going to make sure you are safe."

She knew that was a promise. She could hear it in his voice. "You are very sweet." She ignored the bark of laughter from the peanut gallery. The people he worked with could think calling Kentucky sweet was hilarious all they wanted. But to her he was sweet, and they could just get over themselves. "At some point, I'm going to have to figure out how to do this again." She waved her hands about as she spoke and almost knocked over his coffee mug, which sat on the arm of the swing seat. Thankfully, Kentucky had some fast reflexes and was able to save it. "Sorry."

"Becky, I know you are perfectly capable of looking after yourself." Kentucky was clearly trying to choose his words carefully. If he said she wasn't able to do it right, she was smacking him silly. "This type of thing. This is what we train for. It's what we do, day in, day out. Kicking asshole butt is kinda our jam."

"Truth."

"Damn straight."

"Yup, listen to the boss, Ma'am."

She had no idea who was saying what as they all spoke over each other. While their opinions mattered, there was one person she wanted to hear from. "Caroline?"

"Yes?"

"If it was you…."

"What would I do?"

"Yes."

"I'd let the big lug with that sweet southern drawl sweep me off my feet and take me on vacation to the mountains." Caroline smirked at Wolf when he growled at her words. "And I'd let the others see if they can figure out what's going on while he's keeping you war—um—safe."

What on earth had she been going to say?

"You don't look like you belong in the 'too stupid to live' category," Caroline told her. "So don't end up there."

"You don't pull any punches, do you?"

"Um… no," Caroline replied. "That's not something I've ever been known for."

"Hah." Benny stood out of his chair and stretched his arms over his head. "I'm about to sleep right here in this chair, so if you aren't coming to mine, I'm going to go home and crash."

"Go, go." Crap, she was mortified, it was almost five in the morning. She'd kept these people up all night trying to protect and help her. The least she could do was quit being a ninny and do as they asked. "Thank you for coming to help me."

"Ma'am, we always help family." Benny's voice was serious. "Kentucky is one of us, and that means we'll come on the run every time he calls."

"I—"

"You are his," Benny continued. "That makes you ours and under our protection. If you call, we will come."

"Thank you." She wasn't quite sure what to make of that speech, but that didn't matter. She appreciated they had been so kind. She turned to Kentucky. "Are there bears at Bear Lake?"

"Big Bear Lake," Kentucky corrected. "I don't know, Mozart?"

"No clue, man," Mozart replied. "I just know it's remote and a good place to hide out if need be. I'll make it up there at some point though."

Was she imagining the weird tone in Mozart's voice? She didn't think so. Did he have a problem with Big Bear Lake? But once again, she reminded herself that she was the outsider here. She didn't need to know everything about them all. They had helped her when she'd needed it, and for that she would be forever grateful. Somehow, she would find a way to repay them all for their kindness.

"Then we should think of getting on the road," Kentucky said. "Let the guys go to sleep before Lily and RJ wake up."

"Lily and RJ?"

"My family." Rexar glanced toward the door leading into the house. "They're sleeping in the basement downstairs."

"Why are you still up here?" The words popped out of her mouth before she could stop them. "Get your butt in the house before they think we're keeping you."

"She has spunk, Ken, keep her." Rexar standing up resulted in some of the others following his lead. "Good night." He glanced at the sky, then went into the house.

"I should go, too." Commander Hurt glanced at his watch.

"I'll be just on time for PT if I go now." He got to his feet, gave them a chin lift, and turned toward the side gate.

"Have fun with that." Mozart rubbed two fingers against his temple. "I'm so relieved I'm not on duty today."

"Same." Wolf helped Caroline to her feet. "Why don't you go to bed? I'll fix somewhere for Kentucky and Becky to stay."

"I'll go soon, I promise." Caroline ruffled his hair. "I want to give Becky some stuff, like yoga pants and sweaters. It looks like you guys gave her no time to pack."

Crap, I have no clothes.

"Oh no, I couldn't poss—"

"Shh." Caroline caught her hand and tugged her out of the swing seat. "I have some extras for just this kind of situation. Come with me."

There was no way to say no without upsetting the woman who had been so kind to her. She refused to be that person. "Thank you. I don't know how to say that enough."

"We all have tough days." Caroline led her down a hallway and into a bedroom. "Like one of the boys said a while ago, you are Kentucky's. That makes you family." She pinned her with a look. "In this family, we take care of each other. Today it's you who needs help. Tomorrow it will be someone else. Just pay it forward when you can."

"I promise I will." The only time she'd really seen a family like this was in Montana, so she didn't have a lot to go on, but this kind of family was the one every person should have in their corner. "I will be the person who reaches out. I might not have been that woman very much before. But from now on, I will be."

"That's what this life is all about." Caroline emerged from her closet with some shopping bags. "Helping and being helped. Celebrating together during the good times and having each other's sixes when the bad times roll around."

She plopped the bags on the bed. "I have all sorts of sizes, new still in the package undies, socks, some sports bras, yoga pants, sweats. If you need it, then it's yours."

"It's too much…"

"Not on your Nellie." Caroline tipped the bags out. "You can replace them next time I see you. Consider it a loan if it helps."

"Thank you."

"You're welcome."

"Uh, Caroline?"

"Hm?"

"What does 'not on your Nellie' mean?"

"I heard it on a TV show." The corners of Caroline's mouth quirked up. "*Father Ted*, have you heard of it?"

She shook her head no.

"It's this Irish comedy show about two priests on an island. If you get time to look it up, do. They are hilarious." She grinned. "It helps that I find these off the wall phrases to drive Matthew crazy, as he has to try to decipher them."

"Keeping him on his toes, huh?"

"Damn straight, sister, damn straight."

CHAPTER TWELVE

Kentucky watched the women leave. "You guys can go on home."

"Hell no, sir. Not a chance. Your woman has someone out for her. If you think we are leaving you with no one on your six, you've lost your damn mind."

He'd had a feeling that would be their answer. "It's almost Christmas, you should go home to your families."

"Shut it." Caleb pulled out his phone. "I'm going to find us an Airbnb."

"Find two." The last thing he wanted was Becky jumping out of her skin if she stumbled into the kitchen half asleep and found one of them sitting there. "One for me and Becky, and one for you guys."

"Okay, but I think you're being stupid."

Kentucky was grateful when Draven smacked Caleb on the arm and shook his head as Caleb glanced at him, telling him silently to let it go.

"I'm gonna split," Mozart said. "Kentucky, walk me out to my car, will ya? I have some stuff which might be useful for your trip."

"Sure." He lifted one shoulder when Wolf raised a questioning eyebrow.

No, I have no idea what's going on either.

"What's wrong?"

"Nothing." Mozart walked to his car and hit the button to unlock it. "How much do you know about me?"

"I know you're one hell of an operator and you can't sing for shit," Kentucky quipped and grinned when Mozart narrowed his eyes as if he was trying to figure out the meaning behind the comment. To be fair, they hadn't spent much time together over the years unless it had been on a mission. It would make sense that the other SEAL hadn't put two and two together.

"I have sung exactly one time in my life," Mozart said slowly. "The only way you would know that is if…" He trailed off and glanced at him. "You were there?"

"My mom's bar on karaoke night." Kentucky snickered. "Give someone else a chance to slaughter a song for a while. I might have sort of christened you."

"Asshole." Mozart poked him in the chest. "You are an asshole."

"Could be worse." Kentucky smirked. "I could have called you Dolly or Celine or something. Because if you hadn't shut up, you'd be singing high notes just like those ladies."

Mozart looked sheepish as he acknowledged he was right, there were worse names to have. "True."

He figured he had given Mozart enough shit for now. He'd see if more was warranted after Mozart filled him in. "Why do you want to know how much I know about you?"

Mozart sat into the driver's seat of his car and flipped down the glovebox. He pulled something out and handed it to him. "When I was a teenager, my baby sister was kidnapped and murdered."

Kentucky turned over the card in his hand and saw it was a photo. "Jeez, she was just a baby."

"Avery," Mozart said. "I joined the Navy and became a SEAL, so I can find the bastard who took her away from us."

"Did you find him?"

"No," Mozart admitted softly. "Not yet. But someday I will." He looked Kentucky dead in the eyes. "And when I do, I'm gonna kill him."

"You call me if you need backup." Kentucky wasn't sure where Mozart was going with this, but if he needed him., he'd be there. Period.

"If I give you details on the fucker, will you keep an eye out for him?"

"Of course." Kentucky nodded. "Assholes who do that shit to kids don't deserve to carry on living." A thought snuck in under his skin as Mozart went back to the glovebox. "Do you think he's in Big Bear Lake?"

"I don't know." Mozart handed him a file. "I've followed leads and looked everywhere. But I figured it wouldn't hurt if you could keep an eye out while you are there."

"Anytime, bro." He flipped through the file. "Does Steel not know?"

"They all know." Mozart scrubbed his hand over his hair. "But there's only so many times I can rehash it with them. It's not fair..."

"Cut that shit out," Kentucky ordered. "They are your team, your chosen family. If you want to talk about it with them, do it. It will piss them off if you don't."

"I know," Mozart agreed. "If you see him or hear of him and I'm out of the country, will you let Tex know? He'll get word to me when I get back."

"Tex hasn't been able to find him?" That was weird. Tex could find everyone. He didn't remember a time when Tex had come up blank on a search.

"Not yet."

"You know that could mean this fucker," he shook the file Mozart had given him, "is probably dead, right?"

"I won't stop looking until I know for sure."

Kentucky nodded. He'd do exactly the same. Keep searching and keep looking until he knew for sure that scum was off the streets and the world a slightly safer place to be. "You got it, bro. I'll keep my eyes peeled for him."

"Thanks."

"You're welcome." Instead of shaking the hand Mozart offered, he dragged him into a bro hug and thumped him on the back a couple of times. He'd had no idea Mozart had been dealing with that much shit. If he'd known that when the kid had been singing in his mom's place, he might not have given him the moniker. But he was kinda glad he hadn't known, as he couldn't think of another name which would suit Sam Reed as much as Mozart did.

"Go get your woman," Mozart told him. "Take her somewhere safe, and work on fixing the sad look in her eyes."

"That's exactly what I'm planning on doing."

"Good." Mozart grinned at him. "I can't wait to see her giving you shit and leading you around by the balls."

"Me, too." He wanted that. For Becky to find her sparkle and give him shit when he needed it. "There will come a day when she's calling me saying I did a thing, and I'm not gonna know if that means she caught a skunk in a bucket or shot a hole in the wall."

"She will." Mozart lowered his voice when the other guys came through the gate from the back of the house. "She survived hell. Life is pretty damn sweet when you come out the other side of that shit."

While he appreciated Mozart trying to reassure him, they both knew life didn't always work the way people hoped for. But he planned on doing everything in his power to ensure

Becky had the chance to live the life she should have. He could only hope she'd include him in that life. "I'm going to see where Becky is," he said. "We need to get on the road."

"The bedroom is straight down at the end of the hallway." Wolf nodded to the house. "Just be sure to let the girls know you are approaching, or my Ice will throw something at you, and if you piss her off, I might have to kill you."

He winced. From what he knew of Caroline Steel, that thing she'd be throwing would definitely have the potential to do damage. She'd almost single-handedly taken down a bunch of terrorists who'd attempted to hijack a plane. Wolf might be proud as all get out of his wife, but Kentucky had exactly zero doubts the man would also go balls to the wall to protect her without a second thought. "You got it."

CHAPTER THIRTEEN

Becky rubbed at her eyes. She could tell by how dry and sore they were that she needed to sleep. Not in a car, but in a bed with the biggest fluffiest pillows she could buy.

That would just be a waste of money you don't really have to spend. Sleeping isn't something you do very much of.

Just because I don't sleep well doesn't mean I wouldn't appreciate the heck out of a comfy bed.

"You're thinking mighty hard over there."

"Wha—?" She'd been so lost in her own thoughts she jumped when Kentucky spoke. "Sorry, I was away in my own world."

"Want to tell me about it?"

"I—" She sucked in a breath and let it out slowly. "I was thinking about beds and how I can't wait to sleep on a bunch of the biggest fluffiest pillows I can find."

"You were, huh?"

"Yeah." She shifted the seat belt, so it didn't dig into her neck when she rested her head against the frame of the car door and turned to watch his profile as he drove. "I miss fluffy pillows and being able to relax in a comfy bed."

"We'll fix that just as soon as we can," he promised. "Maybe Santa will leave some... what did you call them? Fluffy pillows under the tree for you."

Oh, crap, it is almost Christmas. What am I meant to do about presents?

"Stop it."

That was an order for sure. She'd heard Kentucky dishing them out to the guys he worked with often enough to recognize the tone. "Stop what?"

"Stop thinking you need presents." He slowed the truck down and pulled as close to the edge as he could to allow a tractor trailer to pass them. "Spending Christmas with you is present enough."

"Sure." She didn't believe that for one second. "We are going to need to stop at a store. Because we are going to need Christmas cookies and goodies." Baking, she could do. It had been a hot minute. "This place we are going to has an oven... right?"

"Caleb called it a tiny house with everything from the kitchen to a full bath. So I think it should have an oven." He pointed to his phone, which he used as a GPS. "We should be there in about five minutes. We'll see what it has for sure when we get there."

"Okay. I'm telling you right now, I'm not awesome at cooking over an open fire. In fact, I suck at it. If the kitchen doesn't have an oven, then you are on cooking duties."

"Deal." He tapped her hand with one finger. "If you want me to stay in the other house with the guys, I can do that."

"No." She shook her head. "I want you to stay with me. Please don't leave me there alone."

"You got it." Following instructions from the GPS lady, he slowed down, flipped on the flicker, and turned them off the road onto a dirt track which had been shoveled clear of snow. "I think we are here."

She peered out the window as they came around a curve in the driveway and the property came into view. Beautiful A-frame cabins were built in a semi-circle. "Wow, it's like a postcard."

Kentucky pulled the truck to a stop in front of the office building. "Yeah, Caleb picked well. I'll have to thank him for not putting us in a dumpsite which moonlights as a camping or glamping site later."

"Definitely." She appreciated that they hadn't ended up in a sketchy place, too. "I think it's pretty."

"Do you want to come in with me to get the key, or will I leave the truck on for you?"

"I'm going to stand outside and breathe some snowy air." It didn't typically get warm in southern California, but here in the mountains with a layer of snow on the ground, she couldn't resist. "I don't remember the last time I was around snow."

He switched off the engine and smiled at her. "Then you have fun in the snow, and I'll check us in."

"Okay, but bring a receipt so I can pay you back for my share." Her bank cards and everything would have to be replaced. But she would call the bank just as soon as they were open after the holidays. Until then, she had resigned herself to mooching off Kentucky. It sucked, but she'd learned over the last few months that she couldn't always do everything herself. Sometimes it was acceptable to take a helping hand when it was offered.

"Don't even go there," Kentucky warned. He opened the rear door of the truck and pulled out his coat. "Put this on so you don't get cold."

I'm not a child.

But she swallowed down the words. Kentucky didn't deserve her bull crap because she was embarrassed to have walked out of her house with nothing but the clothes on her back. He was being his usual self and trying to look out for her. "Thank you." She slid her hands into the arms of the down-lined denim jacket and wrapped the front around herself.

"I'll be back in a minute."

Either he didn't notice her mood or he was actively ignoring it. Possibly even a little of both, if how his jaw tightened was any indication. She couldn't blame him; she was acting like a spoiled brat. She lowered her chin into the jacket and was engulfed by the comforting scent of Irish Spring soap and something she'd come to recognize as uniquely Kentucky. If she could figure out how to bottle it, women across the globe would pay her billions to have it.

It would be unfortunate to have to figure out where to put all the bodies when I murder all those women for wanting to smell like my Tuck, though.

He isn't yours.

I don't care, let a girl dream for five minutes before you go bursting her bubbles. Dang it.

She turned in a slow circle, taking in the trees. The cabins, which were about twelve feet apart, all had cute little porches.

"Do you like it?"

"Yes, it's beautiful." She spun toward him. "Can you imagine sitting on one of those rockers with a mug of hot chocolate and the silence of the snow falling in the middle of the night?"

"The second it snows again, we'll make that happen," Kentucky promised. He opened the back hatch of the truck and grabbed his go-bag and the travel case Caroline had lent her. "We're in number five." He nodded past the end of the office building. "The guys have one and three. So, there's an empty one between each of us."

"We're the only people here?" Her feet crunched through

the snow. She didn't care what anyone else thought, to her, the sound of the ice layer on top of the snow snapping under her feet was one of the happiest sounds on the planet.

"Yes." Kentucky placed their bags next to the front door of their cabin and unlocked the door. "The owners are leaving to go visit family this afternoon. We are the only people here into the new year."

"Is it ridiculous that I want to bounce like a toddler and shout yay?" She hurried to reassure him, "Not that I mind having the guys around. But I like the idea of there not being strangers around for a bit." She paused on the top step and smiled up at him.

"I agree." He took first one big step and then a smaller one until he was directly in front of her. "I'm going to pick you up."

She appreciated the advance warning, but still yelped in surprise when he scooped her into his arms. "What are you doing?"

"This is the first house we've lived in that's just the two of us, so I'm carrying you across the threshold."

"You're crazy." She looped her arms around his neck. "That's meant to be after you get married."

"Doll face, I don't need a piece of paper to call you mine and carry you through the damn door." He nudged the door with his boot and carried her into the living room with a small kitchen area on the left.

"Oh, it's so pretty."

"You sure are."

She wriggled to get down. "I was talking about the room." She was going to ignore how good it felt to slide down his body like that. So good she could almost hear her girly bits yelling that for this man, they were more than a little tempted to go searching for that proverbial key they'd thrown away all those months ago.

"I totally wasn't."

Where the hell had he been hiding the teasing streak he had? Or was this a new development since she'd moved down to California? She smiled up at him and wandered over to the kitchen area while he closed the door, shutting them inside the tiny house.

A tiny house that's even smaller when he's in it.

"We can either run out tonight and grab some groceries, or it can wait until the morning." Kentucky leaned one shoulder against the wall.

She pottered about in the kitchen area, opening and closing cupboards. Pottering was totally her jam. She did an internal fist bump when she found a mixing bowl and utensils. "Awesome, they have a hand mixer. I can make some goodies with this and the oven."

"It works for you?"

She turned in a circle, much like she had outside with her arms out. "Yes. Yes, it does." Impulsively, she stepped into his arms and pressed a kiss to his jaw. "Thank you."

"I can't take credit for finding this place." He cupped her face with one hand, his thumb stroking over her cheek. "That's all on Caleb. But this is all me." He ran his nose along hers before capturing her lips.

She stiffened, waiting for the pain which would follow. Instead, as his lips brushed over hers, once, twice, and then a third time, she found warmth, softness, and a tenderness, she felt to the depths of her soul. She sighed against his lips and he took total advantage of her open mouth to sweep his tongue inside, sipping and tasting at her lips. Her breath hitched softly when he pulled back and pressed another kiss to her cheek. "Wow."

"Yeah." He gave her a brief hug and stepped back. "Wow about fits it."

She touched her lips with the tips of her fingers. "You stopped…"

"You aren't ready, doll face." How the heck did he know that? "When you are, then stopping will be the last thing either of us wants to do."

CHAPTER FOURTEEN

"Do—" He cleared his throat, not because he was trying to hide the effect she had on him from her, but because he didn't mind her knowing it. "—How about we check out the rest of the house?" From where they stood in the kitchen area, they could see everything except what was behind a closed door toward the back of the house. He was guessing that was probably a bathroom. A small table with a set of four chairs sat in the corner on the opposite side of the front door.

Becky ran her hand over a throw blanket on the couch, which ran along the side wall above the table and chairs. "It's so soft."

His mom always watched TV snuggled under a blanket on the couch, as did the other women at the ranch, so he was going to take a wild ass guess and figure it was a girl thing. "Good, that will be cozy to snuggle under and watch TV."

"Wait… men do that, too?"

"Hah, nope. Unless it's a Woobie blanket."

"What's a Woobie blanket when it's at home?"

"It's a poncho liner that's made by constructing two layers

of nylon ripstop fabric. The layers are quilted together with polyester insulation in between." He moved his bag to the end of the couch, picked up hers, and nodded to the stairs which led to a loft. "They are warm and comfy when we're away from home."

"Kinda like the military's version of a security blankie?"

"You're not wrong." He followed her up the stairs to the loft. While he was around, he'd carry her bags and shit. "Some smartass started calling it a Woobie after the kids' blanket in that movie, *Mr. Mom*, and it stuck." He watched her scanning the room and saw the second she realized there was only one bed. "I'm sleeping downstairs," he reassured her. "You are sleeping up here."

"What?"

"You get the bed. I get the couch."

"I'm shorter than you. I should take the couch."

"Never gonna happen, doll face." She could argue with him all she wanted. He was taking the couch, and she got the bed. "Do you want to nap before we go to the store?"

She huffed in annoyance and he freaking loved it. Having her not afraid to show him he'd pissed her off was a start. She didn't deserve to be afraid of her own shadow. If she could be this way with him, hopefully it wouldn't take her long to remember the person she'd been before she'd been taken. He couldn't wait to see that woman shine through the mask she wore. Because now, even with how reserved she was, she called to his soul. When she figured out she could be herself… she was going to blow his damn mind. He just knew it.

She glanced at the silver watch she wore on her wrist. "It might be better to go to the store now and get what we need," she said. "That way we can settle in and we won't have to go out when the stores are packed full of people."

He didn't think there would be that many people in a

store up here on Big Bear Lake, but it was almost Christmas, and he wasn't familiar with the area, so what did he know? "If you want to shower or change, I'll run over and tell the guys in case they want to come, too." He already knew they would come. There wasn't a hope of him taking Becky to the store without having the guys on his six. But he figured she didn't need to know it was because they wanted to protect her and not because they needed food.

"Okay." She followed him down the stairs. "I'll probably just splash water on my face. I can shower before we go to sleep."

He felt his Adam's apple bob up and down as he swallowed around the lump which appeared out of nowhere in his throat. "Um—just make sure that's a bathroom." He pointed to the door at the back of the house, then watched her butt as she went to do as he asked.

She opened the door and leaned in. "It is, and it has a tub."

He didn't care if it had a freaking cat playing a trumpet. If it put a smile on her face like the one she just sent him… he'd cheerfully make sure every bathroom she had to visit had a cat playing a damn trumpet. "Awesome. I'll go over and let the guys know we're gonna go out."

"I'll be here." She trotted up the stairs to where they'd left her stuff. "I forgot to grab my wash bag."

"I'll be back in a few." He barely heard her yell 'see ya' before he was closing the door behind him. He paused and glanced up at the snow-laden clouds. "Give me the strength to be the man she needs."

"You talking to yourself, old man?"

"Fuck you, Draven." He scowled at his asshole friend. "We're gonna go to the store for some shit. You all coming?" He phrased it as a question, but he knew Draven wouldn't take it as one.

“I was just coming over here to ask you guys the same question.”

“Caleb looked in the fridge and realized it was empty except for a pint of milk, right?”

“You said it, bro.” Draven turned away. “I’ll go light a fire under his ass.”

“Thanks.”

“We’ll drive,” Draven called over his shoulder. “You look after your lady, make sure she’s solid.”

“I intend to, bro. I fully intend to.”

* * *

WHAT ON FUCKING earth possessed him to think it was a good idea to go to the store with Caleb and fucking Draven? “Stop that,” he hissed at the latter.

“I’m not doing anything.” Draven moved his hands as if he was conducting an orchestra. “If people don’t want me to try shit, then the boxes shouldn’t say ‘try me’ now, should they?”

“He’s not wrong.”

Kentucky scowled at the stranger who stood behind them. “Don’t encourage him, sir, he’s worse than a four-year-old as it is.”

“Nu-uh.” The man winced. “I have two of those at home, and trust me, he doesn’t even come close.” He waved at them and called over his shoulder, “Happy Holidays.”

“Merry Christmas, sir.”

“Do you think we have enough?” Becky stepped around Draven and his singing toy musical performance and dropped an armful of tinsel and baubles into the cart. “Who knew Bert and Ernie would still sound the same after all these years?”

“Because someone has forgotten that some of us actually grew up.” He nodded to the cart. If it overflowed, he’d send their two troublemakers to go grab a second one. "Do you want more?"

"Umm..."

"Tell me?"

She leaned in close to him and whispered in his ear, "Do you think we could persuade the men-children to make decorations with popcorn, paper, and string?"

"Hell yes." If they had something to do with their hands, it might keep them out of trouble. "It's just a damn shame we can't get them started here. It might prevent us from getting kicked outta the store before we get to pay." If that happened, he was going to boot their asses and make them run all the way home, like that momma on Tickle Tock did when her kid was an ass to a lady running. "Becky?"

"Yes?"

"Will you grab me a fresh notebook and pen, please? I forgot to grab mine out of my go-bag, and I need to write something down in case I forget it."

"Oh, oh." Becky grinned at him. "We can't have you without a notebook, that will never do." He winced when she stopped in front of a shelf filled with notebooks. "They have pink, purple, neon green, or neon yellow."

"No black?"

She flipped through the notebooks and shook her head over her shoulder. "No black."

Damn it.

"Blue then, please."

"With glitter?" She held up one palm sized notebook, and then a second one. "Or without?"

"With," Draven called. "Always with glitter."

"Shut up," he hissed the order. "Without please, Becky." He glared at Draven. "I'm going to murder you and feed you to the sharks out by La Jolla without salt, asshole." He took the notebook Becky offered him and fumbled in his pockets for a pen and came up empty. "Shit."

"Looking for one of these?" Becky produced a package of pens from behind her back.

"Yes, please." He didn't even care that they hadn't been paid for yet. He opened the package, took out a pen, and scribbled a note into the book.

Kilkenny: 150 laps and 500 sit-ups for being a dick at the store. Hunt: Same for abandonment to guard the truck and leaving me as supervisor to the toddler asshole.

"I COULD MAYBE DO ONE A MONTH," Becky whispered. "If you asked me to do all of those in one sitting, I'm telling you now, have an ambulance on standby, k?"

"You…" He tugged her close to press a kiss to her temple, "…aren't an asshole like my dumbass brother is."

"Phew." She wiped her fingers across her forehead. "I was starting to freak out there, just a bit."

He glanced at her out of the corner of his eye as they walked down the aisle. If he hadn't been watching her so closely, he might never have seen the slight downward turn of her lips and the tightness in her forehead. She was putting up one hell of a good front. "Are you ready to go?"

"Yeah, I think I have everything."

"Then let's go check out." He turned and whistled. When Draven looked at him, Kentucky pointed to the front of the cart. "Hold onto that and help us drive it. It's heavy."

"Yes, sir."

Murder is wrong and jail doesn't have good coffee.

Murder is wrong and jail doesn't have good coffee.

Murder is wrong and jail doesn't have good coffee.

Maybe if he repeated it enough in his head, they could make it through the checkout with Draven Kilkenny still breathing. Kentucky had better plans than jail for the next few days than to spend time figuring out how to get bailed out when everything was shut down for the holidays.

CHAPTER FIFTEEN

Shopping with the guys had been an experience she wasn't sure she'd been quite ready for. Someone could have warned her they were exhausting. Not that she'd minded stopping at the first roadside stall. The pumpkin spice latte had been welcome. But they'd also stopped for roasted chestnuts, then again for popcorn, and if that wasn't enough, then Caleb had insisted they also needed some hot cider.

"How are you doing, doll face?"

"If he doesn't hurry up and get us back to the house," she said dryly, "he'll be mopping up the seats back here for a month."

Kentucky had just taken a mouthful of coffee and she didn't even feel bad that he spewed it all over the back of Draven's head.

"Hey. What the hell, asshole?" Draven swiped at his hair and scowled at his hand when it came away wet. "Did you just spit all over me?"

"Payback for making every fucking toy in the store make noise."

"I told you." Caleb paused to let a bunny rabbit get across

the road. "Rexar does the same shit, and I made the mistake of going with them to a store last month when we were getting stuff for Rory's kid. I'm never making that mistake again."

"You could have warned me," Kentucky growled. "I'd have made him stay in the damn truck, and you could have come in the store."

"I didn't say I wouldn't do the same thing." Caleb took the turn off for the cabins. "But I figure I have enough exercise planned for me in your book already that I didn't need to go adding to it today."

"Shit." Draven leaned around to glare at Kentucky. "Did you seriously…? What am I saying? Of course you did. Asshole."

Don't think about peeing. It will go away. Think about how they are like a bunch of little boys in the classroom you used to have. All squabbles and arguing, but backing each other up if anyone outside their tight-knit group says something weird to one of them.

Caleb must have hit every freaking pothole on purpose. Every single one reminded her bladder that it had urgent needs. She squeezed her eyes shut and tried to concentrate on something else, anything else. But could she even remember the words to a single nursery rhyme? No. No, she couldn't. Finally, Caleb stopped the truck in the parking spaces in front of the office building. "I'll open the door if you give me the keys."

"I got it, babe."

Damn him for not reading my mind.

She silently thanked the bladder gods for being kind to her when she was able to help them carry the bags to the house without her muscles failing at their job. That was a little more embarrassment than she was willing to deal with right now and she was more than certain that the guys would be, too, if they knew the situation.

"Where the hell did that come from?"

She couldn't see around Kentucky to see what on earth he was talking about. But he was between her and the door, so he nudged him in the back with her elbow, silently pleading with him to hurry his butt up. "Where did what come from?"

"The tree in a pot." Kentucky finally stepped up onto the porch and she was able to see the small spruce fir in a black pot which sat next to the front door.

"We have one, too, Ken." Caleb pointed to their cabin. "What's the note say?"

"What note?"

"The one staring you in the face."

Becky stepped to one side to make room for Caleb to move past her. Could they hurry this up? Seriously, her bladder was going to explode if…

Flip it.

She petted Kentucky's back, letting him know she was there, and slid her hand down to run over his butt, feeling for the shape of the key. She slid her hand into the ass pocket of his pants when she thought she'd found it. "Don't mind me."

"What are you doing?"

"Looking for the house key."

"This one?" Kentucky opened the button on the top pocket of his coat and fished out a key with a large size keyring. "Why didn't you ask?"

She was not going to answer that right now. She had much more urgent things to see to. She snatched the key from his hand, opened the door, and raced for the bathroom.

I'm never, ever drinking pumpkin spice anything a-freaking-gain.

Mortified didn't even begin to describe how embarrassed she was. She'd known better than to drink it. Every damn time she had something with cinnamon in it, this happened. She finished what she had to do—the relief almost as awesome as removing her bra after a long day at work—and ran the faucet to wash her hands. Over the sound of the running water, she heard the sound of first one phone and then another, swiftly followed by a third phone ringing. She knew before even going out there that this wasn't a good thing. She dried her hands, walked out of the bathroom, and glanced from one to the other. "What's wrong?"

"The guys have to leave," Kentucky told her the obvious, as both Caleb and Draven were already outside the front door.

"And you aren't?" This couldn't be normal. "What's wrong? What happened?" If he couldn't tell her, she'd have to understand it. But something told her this was a normal *job* for them.

"Caroline and Rexar's son have been kidnapped."

"And you aren't going?" He was staying here for her and she would not allow it. "Caroline and that little boy are missing."

Kentucky scrubbed his hand from back to front over his head. She didn't need to be a genius to see this was killing him. "I know."

Suddenly, reality slammed into her, and she just knew. "You are worried shackles asshole will come for me when you are gone." He hesitated. Only for a split second, but enough for her to catch it. "Did he follow us?" She was so scared out of her mind that shackles dick would show up too. But there wasn't a chance in apples that she was going to tell Kentucky that.

"I don't know."

"Then get your ass out that door." She pointed to where the other two were watching them, much as one would a tennis match. "If he comes back, I survived before. I'm stronger than I look, and I swear I'll be alive if you have to come find me again. Go get that baby and Caroline back."

"Fucking hell."

"I agree, they could be taken into fucking hell." Oh, she could tell this was killing him. But there was no fucking way she was letting him stay here with her. If something went wrong, he'd never forgive himself and she wouldn't allow that to happen. "You need to go help get them back." Out of the corner of her eye she saw Draven disappear and from when she'd stayed with them in Montana, she knew he was probably going to load weapons into the truck. "Leave me a truck and a phone and go." She went to him and wrapped her arms around him, snuggling into his chest. "It's the right thing to do."

"I know." He sighed against her hair. "I need for you to be safe, too."

"If the assholes don't know where I am, I will be." All she could do was promise him something, which they both knew had the potential to be a lie.

"I'll leave you my phone," he said finally. "Speed dial one is for Trev at HQ, and I'll program Tex's number into speed dial two."

"If you put Willow's number in speed dial three, I'll be golden." She watched him tapping at the numbers. "I'm going to bake and call her for some virtual girl time. It's probably better that you aren't here under my feet. I'll get a lot more cookies baked if you all aren't helping yourselves as the cookies come out of the oven."

The look on Kentucky's face said he didn't believe one single bit of her bravado. "Are you sure?"

"Yes, I promise. Now go."

"Okay." He handed her the phone, then turned and took three steps toward the door before coming back to her and smacking a fast kiss on her lips. "Be safe."

"I swear." Wasn't she meant to be the one telling him that? "Look after each other. I—be safe."

With a wave, he climbed into the truck with the others and took off down the drive. Now what was she supposed to do? Fear engulfed her, and she dropped heavily onto the couch. Fear for Caroline. For the little boy she had yet to meet. Fear for the guys. Rage that shit things could happen to good people and there wasn't anything she could do about it. Not one single thing, but wait. "Waiting freaking sucks." The phone in her hand buzzed a second before the music joined in and she swiped the screen to answer the call. "Hello?"

"Girl, hi, how are you doing?"

"Hey, Willow." How did she know Becky needed to hear a friendly voice right now? Was her friend reading her mind all the way from Montana? If so, then she would totally like to be gifted with that skill, too, please. "How are you?"

"Kentucky called Cormack," Willow said.

She has got to be reading my mind.

"I figured I'd call," Willow continued. "Because I remember how I was the first time Cormack went out after we got together. I was a mess, and I was used to it with my dad."

"Yeah, but your dad going to work is totally different than sending your man out the door and not knowing if he's going to come back or not." There it was, he wasn't her man. But she really wished he was.

"You are part of an elite club now, sister," Willow said. "Loving these men isn't something everyone can do. Actually, I lie. Loving them is easy. Dealing with their lifestyle, their jobs, their closed mouths, and dangerous activities without going insane… that's the hard bit."

"So I'm finding out."

"Hah, I knew it. You love him?"

"What? No." She needed something to do. She'd allow

Willow to tie her up in knots if she didn't. "I'm going to put you on speakerphone and unpack the groceries while we talk, if that's okay?"

"Sure, go right ahead," Willow replied. "I'm making cookies."

"That's the plan for me, too." She put the phone on the counter and started emptying shopping bags onto the tables. "Although I have no recipes, so I hope I can remember the measurements or there will be no cookies when they get back."

"I have my iPad here, too. I can look them up while we talk."

"Awesome, thank you." She refused to believe that they wouldn't find Caroline and the little boy. "What's Rexar's son's name? I know it was mentioned, but my brain is scattered…"

"RJ." Over the phone, the sounds of utensils clattering filtered through. "His name is RJ."

She guessed he must have been named after his father. "RJ."

"Did their boss's wife have her baby?" She was sure she remembered that as being part of the conversation last night. But she was running on so little sleep, it was also possible she'd made it up.

"Oh my God, Becks." Willow laughed so hard Becky was sure her belly had to hurt. "Uncle D was hilarious. He raced in here in a mad panic, looking for the hospital go-bag. Hands flapping, running around like a headless chicken, only for them to get to the hospital and be told it's a false alarm and they had to come home again."

"Tell me you got that on video?" She'd met the head of Nemesis Inc. and he hadn't struck her as the kind of guy to lose his mind. Apparently, she'd been mistaken. "Because I need to see your Uncle D freaking out like that."

"I don't," Willow admitted. "I was too busy holding onto the railing on their porch trying to stop myself from laughing in his face."

"Dang it, Willow."

"But I know Trev got it on the security cameras," Willow said. "I'll have Cormack send it to Kentucky's phone when they get back."

That little nugget of information told her Dalton and Cormack were on route, too. "Thank you." It made her feel a little better to know the same bunch of badasses who'd been part of her rescue were coming to help. Her phone pinged and she pulled her head out of the fridge to glance at it.

"I sent you a screenshot of my recipe for shortbread cookies," Willow explained the message tone. "We can dip them in melted chocolate if you have some."

"I do, and I have a gigantic bag of candy." She frowned at the one remaining shopping bag she had to empty. "As in, Draven insisted we needed a seven-pound bag of mini bars of chocolate."

"Awesome. We'll make those into cookies, and he can whine all about it until Kentucky pulls out his scribble book. Then he'll really have something real to whine about," Willow said. "Get your utensils together, sister, and let's bake."

"You sound like we're on one of those TV shows." She decided this friend was a friend for all seasons. Willow didn't have to spend her evening on the phone with her. She didn't have to include her as if she was a significant other of one of the men, yet here she was dishing out orders like a chef on crack.

"Hah." Willow snorted. "I'm in the kitchen at alpha house. If you hear grumbling, it's Kace bitching that I'm underfoot when really he's just waiting to see if I use my baking skills for good or bad tonight."

"I heard that," a muffled male voice she recognized as belonging to Nemesis Inc's chef replied.

"Shoo, Kace," a woman's voice said. "Unless you are a wife or the partner of an operator, your butt does not belong in this kitchen tonight."

"That's Lina. She and the girls just walked in," Willow said. "We're making Christmas cookies, and next year, Becky, your butt better be in this kitchen with us."

"But I might not be the wife or partner of an operator?"

"I call bull-crap on that."

"That's Adalyn," Willow told her. "She doesn't swear much. Actually, neither does Eedana, but we're working on corrupting them both."

"The guys swear enough for everyone," Adalyn said. "I don't need my son learning more creative ways to describe how to empty a frick fracking bucket of mush into a feed box."

"Add me to the 'not swearing much' bunch." She searched in the drawers, looking for measuring cups. If she had to go back to the store to grab some, she was going to be annoyed with herself for not thinking about checking if she had them earlier. "I was a teacher for way too long to have made it a habit. If I'd slipped up in class and brought out my pirate mouth, I'd have been before the school board before I'd finished speaking."

"I call bull-crap," Adalyn repeated. "You wouldn't be where you are using Kentucky's phone if he didn't care."

"I know." But there was caring and being part of something bigger. She wasn't sure if that something bigger was possible for her. "Is this something you do when the guys leave for work?"

"Usually we grab goodies and pile up in someone's house to read and binge on treats and wine," Willow replied. "But we need Christmas cookies, and we figured as it's Caroline and RJ, then we should keep our hands busy."

"Oh." It was an awesome idea. She wondered if Caroline and the other women did the same.

Shit. Who's looking after Fiona and Alabama if Caroline is the one missing?

"You sucked in a breath so loud that we could hear you all the way from here. What's wrong?" Lina asked. "Do I need to send backup?"

"No—um—I'm okay. Sorry. I just wondered if this was something Caroline and her girlfriends did and if they were okay."

"I don't have a number for any of them," Lina replied. "I can go ask Trev."

"You are not moving from this kitchen," Willow said. "I see how you are wincing every time you move. If you drop that baby before Uncle Dalton gets back, he's going to be all kinds of pissed that he missed it."

"I promise to keep my legs crossed until his boots hit the deck."

"That's not how it works, Mamba. You stay put. I'll go ask Trev."

"What if I called Tex?" She figured now was a good time to interrupt. "Tuck programed his number into his phone for me, too."

"She calls him Tuck," someone cried. "That's so awesome. Becky and Tuck."

"Tucky."

"Bucky."

"Bucky, I love it."

They were talking over each other so fast she had no idea who was saying what. But it was official, as far as she was concerned, these women had lost their minds. "You are not using that name. Ever." Oh my god, if this was like the names the guys used. Call signs, nicknames, or whatever they were. She was going to lose her freaking mind. She needed to change the subject, and she needed it to happen fast before they decided she and Kentucky were a flipping Bucky. "I'm going to try to call Tex and see if he can hook us up with Fiona and Alabama." She glared at the butter in her hand. It would need to be softened before she could use it. "As long as nobody minds?"

"Nope. Go ahead," Lina replied for everyone. "If Dalton has an issue with it, I'll tell him I have baby brain or something."

"Okay. Gimme a second and I'll call you back."

CHAPTER SIXTEEN

Tex didn't take his eyes off the screen as he tapped at the ringing phone next to him. "Tell me you got something."

"Um—hi?"

"What the heck?" He tapped pause on the traffic footage he was watching and picked up the phone. "Who is this?"

"Am—um—Kentucky said I should call you..."

"What's wrong? Are you okay?" Fuck, he pulled up a chat box he'd kept open to relay information to Wolf and tucked the phone under his ear so he could type out a message. "Do you need backup? Where are you?" He asked the rapid-fire questions before he remembered this woman wasn't used to him or how he worked. "Do you need help?" He had no freaking clue who he had in that area, but he would find someone or send Kentucky back if he had to. Then he remembered he hadn't introduced himself. "Hello, Becky, I'm Tex. But you probably know that."

"I'm okay." She cleared her throat. "I was talking to my friends in Montana." She hesitated before continuing. "You know the ones whose men are out working? Oh, and hi, Tex."

"Hi. Yes, I know of them," he said.

He hadn't a clue where this was going, but he figured if she was calling him, there was a reason for it.

"While we were getting ready to bake Christmas cookies together..."

How the heck were they going to bake together when they were miles apart? "Wait, they are there with you?" Dalton Knight would lose his shit if his very pregnant wife skipped her happy ass down to California when she was meant to be home safe in Montana.

"No, no." The more she spoke, the less Tex could hear the shake in her voice. "We were all on a call," she explained. "But then I was thinking about Fiona and Alabama, that's their names... right?"

"Yes, Abe's and Cookie's women."

"I didn't meet them," Becky replied. "But I wondered if they have someone to bake Christmas cookies with while they wait. I don't have their numbers, but I thought you might have and be able to give them mine so they can join in. If they want to, that is."

He almost didn't understand the words as they were coming out of her mouth so fast. But once he did, his heart stuttered. This was a good woman; she was concerned about two other women she had never met and wanted to include them in making Christmas cookies just because she didn't want them to go through the weeds of having a friend missing alone.

Smith chose well. Becky is freaking awesome.

This right here was why he did the job he did. Because decent people *did* exist. "Do you want me to call them and ask, or just give them your number and let them decide?"

"If there is a way to do a group call or something. I don't know, tech isn't my thing, which is why I called you."

"You got it." Tex's brain was already running through the

possibilities. "Let me send Trev a message and call the girls. I'll call you back in ten, okay?"

"Okay. Thank you," Becky replied. "As long as it doesn't cause problems for the job you are working on. That's priority number one."

"I know. I won't let anyone down," Tex promised her. "I'll call you back on this number in ten minutes. Make sure you answer it, okay?"

"Okay. Bye."

"Bye, Becky. Thank you for thinking of this and for calling me to help." The phone in his ear went dead, and he opened another chat box. If he knew anything about Trev, his ears were reserved for the comms units his guys were no doubt using.

Tex: I need…

He paused mid-type. Shit, he should find out if the girls wanted to do this first before he got with Trev to find out if they could group call on Nemesis Inc.'s phones. He picked up his phone again and pressed the number he needed, then put it to his ear.

"Have you heard anything? Are they okay? Did you find them?"

"Shh, Fee, Calm." He hated hearing the fear and worry in Fiona's voice yet a-freaking-gain. "Not yet. But did Caroline tell you about Becky, Kentucky's woman?"

"Yes, does she want to come over? Where should we go to pick her up?"

These women were so damn awesome. The men may be teams and brothers in arms, but the women they had chosen as life partners were just as amazing at looking after the other wives and girlfriends. "No, she's up at Big Bear Lake, but she knows some of the women from Nemesis, and they're doing some Christmas baking over a group call." He heard the confused noise from Fiona. "They wanted to know if you and Alabama wanted to join that call and bake with them."

"Um, I'm not very good at baking," Fiona told him. "But let me ask Alabama. We're at Caroline and Wolf's place. We didn't know what else to do."

"That's okay," he reassured her. "Ice would want you to be there. It's where you always go when the guys have a mission," he reminded her.

"Let me ask Alabama."

He could hear the hushed tones as she did that and waited for their decision. He'd just have to figure out a way to let Becky down gently if that answer was no.

"Yes, but you're going to have to do the joining the calls bit, as neither of us is sure how to do it."

"Deal, give me a minute and I'll get with the tech guy on the other side." He went back to his text box.

Tex: Trev, I need a Zoom call or a group call for the women.

Trev: Huh... what?

He wasn't one bit surprised by that reaction. He'd been able to talk it out with Becky. Trev didn't have that privilege.

Tex: Becky and the women at your HQ are baking Christmas cookies, and I need to patch in Abe's and Cookie's women so they can bake together over the wire.

Trev: That is the weirdest request I have ever gotten.

Trev: Gimme a minute.

"Bet you ten bucks he's calling to wherever the women are to check with them," Tex said to the room. Not that there was anyone there to answer him. He'd have to remember to tell CC_CopyCat about this later. He could leave out the names and locations. She'd get a kick out of these women for sure.

Trev: Here's the Zoom link and passcode.

Tex: Thanks. I'll be back in five.

Trev: I've got comms. The guys are following the route out to the Salton Sea.

Tex: Yeah. I'm checking shit on this side. I'll get the women situated and be back.

Trev: k.

CHAPTER SEVENTEEN

"It was a stupid idea. Tex probably thinks you've lost any marbles you might have possessed at one time." Becky pulled the butter from the microwave and poked at it to see how soft it was before putting it back in for another ten seconds. "It's not stupid if it keeps us sane and the guys don't have to deal with hysterics when they get back." Well, she might be the only one hysterical, but still. "Eeep." She jumped a mile when the phone buzzed at the same time as the microwave beeped. She popped the door on the microwave and picked up the phone. "Hello?"

"Hey, Becky, this is Tex."

"Hi." She held her breath as she waited for him to tell her if Operation Christmas Cookie was a go or not. That was what happened with missions or jobs, right? The guys called them Operation something or other.

"Do you have a pen and paper?" Tex asked. "I have a website I need you to tap into google and then a password to get you into the meeting room… video is okay, right?"

No. No, it wasn't. She was a mess, in clothes she'd been wearing for days, and she couldn't remember the last time her hair had even smelled a brush, never mind met one. But she'd put him to all this trouble to set it up. "Yes, of course." She pulled the notepad from its magnet on the fridge door and a pen from the mug with the broken handle next to the microwave. "Go ahead."

"Ready?"

"Yes." She wrote down the details Tex gave her. "Got it, thank you."

"You're welcome. Call me back if you have any problems logging in."

She could hear a phone ringing on his side and did the only thing she could do. "I will, I promise. Thank you, Tex."

"You're welcome. I gotta go."

She placed the phone on the counter and tapped in the Zoom website he'd given her. "You can do this. Caroline wouldn't like them if they weren't as awesome as she is." She blew out a long slow breath and tapped in the password, but paused before hitting send. She was being ridiculous. This wasn't the school playground. These women weren't bullies, they probably needed the distraction as much as she did. Becky hit send and waited as the screen flipped to the bunch of mini screens. "Uh—hi."

"Becky, you made it." Willow waved from one of the boxes. "We have two screens between us as all four of us won't fit on one phone." She tugged someone by the elbow and another woman popped into view. "This is Adalyn."

"Hi."

"Hey, you." Adalyn waved at her. "You've got this."

How did she know she was so nervous? Did it show on her face? "We've got this."

"Yes, we do." The woman she recognized as Lina sat on a bar stool next to a countertop. "Well, I don't have the baking thing. I'm the official taste tester tonight." She grinned into the screen. "Fiona and Alabama are on screen two."

"Hi."

"Thank you for including us. I'm Fiona, and that's Alabama," the first woman said. "I'm the taste tester on this side, and Alabama is baking. If I set the oven on fire or burn the cookies, then I'll never hear the end of it."

"You'll burn Cookie, alright." Alabama snickered. "I'm sure he won't object."

"Shh, you're so bold right now."

"And that's one of the many reasons we're friends." Alabama hugged Fiona. "Because I remind you to laugh and that you've got this."

"I just figured if we needed it, you did, too." She didn't know these women's stories, but if she had to guess from the haunted look in Fiona's eyes, hers at least was similar to her own. Becky decided right there and then that she would do everything she could to keep Fiona's mind off what was happening right now. "I don't want to be alone right now, but there was no way I was letting Kentucky stay behind just because I was being stupid."

"That word is not allowed," the other woman on screen with Lina interjected. "Stupid is not something we use between us. You aren't allowed to use it for you either."

"Yes, Ma'am."

Crap, I'm screwing up already.

"Hi, I'm Eedana, and Adalyn has been my friend for years." Eedana giggled as Adalyn swatted at her with a tea-towel. "Be aware she writes books, so anything you say or do can and will be used in a future story."

"You're so mean. I don't do that."

They weren't baking so far, but just having these women, all of whom were in a similar position to her, on screen as support and offering friendship was more than she could ever have hoped for.

"So that wasn't you out by the corrals leering at the

cowboys with your notepad and pencil, scribbling down notes as they hauled hay this morning when I was walking Buddha then?" Lina quirked up an eyebrow.

"Damn busybody."

"I…"

"You're either bored or nesting," Adalyn muttered. "I vaguely remember that stage."

"Let's bake." Willow clapped her hands, drawing all their attention away from where Lina was spluttering at Adalyn. She picked up some sheets of paper. "I printed out a ton of recipes. Who wants to pick the first batch?"

"Becky," Fiona said. "It was her idea to bring us all together and do this. She should pick."

"Gingerbread men?"

"You got it." Willow flipped through the pages and picked one before she reached for the phone. "I'm going to upload a recipe so we all have the same one, unless anyone has any family recipes to share?"

After a chorus of no's, Becky's phone pinged, and by the time she'd figured out how to flip from the Zoom call to messages and back again, her nerves had been pushed to the back burner. But flip it, she was an idiot for picking gingerbread men. "I'm going to have to freehand these cookies, these cookie men are going to be all kinds of lopsided."

"Same."

"Make sure you give them a big—"

"Lina," Adalyn warned.

Lina dipped her hand into a bowl and tasted the mixture. "What? I was going to say… um… hat. I was going to say hat, I swear."

"Sure, we believe you, thousands wouldn't," Alabama piped up. And just like that, this entire night was normal. Fun and comforting. "Thank you all for doing this."

"Don't be an idiot." Willow pointed at the screen with a batter covered wooden spoon. "This was an awesome idea."

"If we manage to make cookies and don't need to call the fire brigade, we can feed the guys and Caroline when they get back," Fiona chimed in. "That has to be worth brownie points for sure."

They passed away the hours, baking and chatting. By the time they'd made the gingerbread men which had turned into gingerbread stars as none of their kitchens had the cutters for the men, Italian cookies, and were onto peanut butter clusters, the conversation turned to the guys and the little things they did which mattered. Coffee in the morning, or bringing a hot water bottle for period cramps. Becky had something she needed to ask. "You know that move when you're walking with a man and he slows slightly, rests his palm flat on the small of your back, and bends down so he can still hear you or speak to you?"

"Yes." On screen Fiona put her hand on the oven door, and Alabama tugged it away. "Why is that move so damn hot?" Fiona asked.

"It's not just me then, right?"

"No, Becky, it's all of us." Fiona grinned at the screen and dodged Alabama's swat. "There is something about a man wanting to show us we're important, which is panty-melting hot."

"I'll melt more than your panties if you touch that oven again," Alabama warned. "Those cookies will be soggy in the middle, and none of us want a soggy middle."

OMG, the wine she had just taken a sip out of spewed across the phone. "Jeez, warn a girl, will ya?"

"Oops."

"What a waste of wine." Becky mourned the loss. She'd only found a half bottle which their hosts had left in the fridge. "I'm going to have to go out tomorrow and buy more wine."

"Do you have money?" Willow asked. "I can send you some if you need it. I know you left your place with nothing."

"Crap. I've been having such a good time, I forgot about that."

"We got you, girl," Lina called. "Just tell us what Western Union to send it to and it will be there for you to pick up in the morning."

She refused to feel bad. These women understood. They got it. "I'll pay you back as soon as I can get my bank cards. I'll ask Kentucky to swing by my rental and grab some of my stuff..."

"Sister, if you think he's going to want to lead the bad guys to you, you've lost your mind," Willow added. "Kentucky can send it back to us, or you can pay it forward in the future."

She didn't know what to say. Loss for words wasn't normally a thing for her, but now she had none. Becky shook her head, trying to shake some loose, she refused to look like a gold digger in front of these women. "The insurance my job had keeps paying me for another six months," she explained. "After that I have to figure out what to do, as if I have no money coming in, I'm going to have to go back to work. But for now, I can afford to pay you back or pay it forward."

"We'll figure it out tomorrow." Lina nibbled on the edge of a cookie. "What do you want to do after the insurance stops paying out? You're a teacher, right?"

"Yes."

"I didn't know schools gave that kind of insurance," Fiona said. "At least, I didn't think they did."

"I didn't either," she admitted. "But Kentucky figured it out while we were still there at Nemesis."

"Ah." Willow turned to glance at Lina before turning back

to her again. "Have you looked at teaching English online? There are loads of people who need English lessons."

"Oh, that's an awesome idea." Alabama pulled her tray of Italian cookies out of the oven. "If you do it online, you can target people overseas, too."

"Yes, I agree." Fiona moved their gingerbread stars over on the cooling rack to make room for the hot cookies. "China and Japan especially, as those regions are always looking for English teachers. If you've taught kindergarten, you can deffo teach teenagers and adults."

"I'm not sure. Toddlers are a lot easier to keep on track. Give them a cookie or promise them a nap and they're all in."

"Kinda like the rest of us, then," Eedana quipped. "A nap and goodies, and we're all set."

"Yeah."

"Promise us you'll at least think about it," Willow pushed.

She needed to think about it. Going back to what she did before might not be possible. "I promise. It's a good idea."

"That's good enough for me." Lina picked up a phone and glanced at it. "Hey, Sailor."

Was that Dalton? Every woman on the screens watched Lina.

"You got them?" Lina asked, then glanced at them. "They got them. They're okay. They are on their way back to Wolf's house."

"YES!"

"YAY."

"Thank you, sweet baby Jesus."

Chaos erupted in each of their kitchens. Becky didn't even care that she didn't have someone to hug and dance around with. If anyone but these women had seen her funky ass dancing, she'd have been mortified. "I'm so relieved."

"Clean up, ladies," Willow ordered. "Tired and cranky men will be inbound, stat."

"Thank you all for doing this," Becky said. "Waiting was easier with all of you to wait with me."

"This has got to become a new tradition," Fiona agreed. "Imma going to talk to Caroline about it. I don't care if I'm not a domestic goddess, but I know Hunter will think I am when I feed him cookies."

Will Kentucky think the same of me?

She wasn't sure he would, but she'd better get this kitchen cleaned up… just in case. "Bye, girls."

"See ya."

"Bye."

"We'll call soon."

"Don't swan off to Montana without coming to see us."

"I won't, I promise." She'd only just met most of them, but already they felt like people she wanted to know better. "Bye."

"And this is why you clean as you go." She had left a big mess for herself and had been tempted to just toss everything in the sink to deal with in the morning. She glanced out the window at the snow, which had been falling softly only a few hours ago. Now it was almost a blizzard. She could barely make out the outside lights of the office, which had come on automatically at dusk. "I hope they make it." She grabbed some milk and put it in a pan on the stovetop to heat. Hot chocolate sounded like just the ticket right now, and if she added a splash of the Baileys Caleb had asked for at the store, then it was nobody's business but hers. While she waited for the milk to boil, she ran upstairs to grab the throw blanket off the bed. If she was going outside to watch the snow fall, then she wanted to at least be able to pretend to herself that she was prepared and warm.

A few minutes later she hovered near the front door with a steaming mug of Baileys-laced hot chocolate in her hand and the throw wrapped around her. "There is no one out there." She stared into the dark, trying to make out the shadows which loomed just out of the light thrown by the solar lanterns hanging on the eaves of the porch. If she told herself that enough, maybe she would start to believe it. "This is supposed to be peaceful, dang it." She huffed out an annoyed breath at her nervousness and sighed deeply. "Fine. I'm going back inside to wait for Tuck on the couch."

CHAPTER EIGHTEEN

"Dude, slow the fuck down or we're going over the edge."

Kentucky snorted. "Hang on to the oh shit bar and make sure you don't fall out." He downshifted and hit the gas, coming out of the turn. The back ass of the truck fishtailed and the horses under the hood gave him the power he was looking for. "Snow is coming down fast. We either make it up to Big Bear in the next hour, or we're walking… take your pick."

"I want to make it in one piece." Draven braced himself against the side of the truck and inhaled harshly when the truck skidded, scraping the side on the guardrail. "Slow the fuck down."

"I'm not even doing thirty." Kentucky figured now might be a good time to put the guys out of their misery. "I need the power to make it up around these fucking bends." It had been a stupid idea to leave Becky up here alone. If he had to hike the rest of the way up, he was going to be even more pissed with himself than he already was. Never mind the guys who would give him shit about it for months. But did he care? No, no, he didn't.

"Man, if I die on Christmas Eve," Caleb muttered, "my mom is going to haunt you for life. That's if you survive what Snow will do to you if you make it out alive."

"You can tell all y'all didn't take the defensive driving course in Switzerland that Nem offered us a few years ago." He eased up on the gas and almost immediately, the engine struggled. "I need the fucking power."

"Then drive in the middle of the fucking road," Draven advised.

"And get creamed by some dude running from the snow who I can't see coming around the next bend? No fucking thanks." Jeez, he'd be willing to bet a full tray of the cookies Tex said Becky had been baking that if it was their women up at the cabin alone and mother nature was dropping ten feet of snow along the route in a once in a lifetime mega storm, they'd be telling him to drive faster. Hopefully, his memory hadn't decided to fail him and around the next bend was a flat piece of road so he could give the truck some more gas again. "How much have we left to go?"

Draven glanced at the GPS unit which by some miracle hadn't given out yet. "About fifteenish miles."

"Thank fuck. That's walkable." For every bend they took and every mile they got closer was one less they'd have to walk when they wiped out. Because even with his skills, he knew that was more than likely going to happen at some point.

"Yeah," Draven muttered. "But I'm telling you right now, I'm going to bitch at you the whole fucking way."

"What's new?" Caleb snorted. "You are the queen of bitching."

"That's prince of bitching to you, asshole."

Kentucky tuned them out to focus on the road. He didn't even dare take one hand to rub at his temples. The headache which raged behind his eyes would normally require painkillers, but in this snow, he didn't dare take anything.

"Ten miles," Draven informed him.

Easy day—I can walk ten miles in my sleep.

He peered through the swishing wipers just in time to make out the faint glow of headlights coming straight toward him and hugged the guardrail as much as he could. "Damn it, you're too close, asshole." Only years of experience of unexpected loud noises going off near him kept him from slamming on the brakes when the battered pickup took off the wing mirror right next to him. "Shit." He wasn't fucking stopping. He'd pay for the damn mirror to be fixed or let Nemesis use the top-notch insurance he always insisted on taking for rentals.

"Shiiit!" Draven yelped.

"Yeah."

"You aren't stopping?"

"Not a fucking chance in hell," he muttered. "If I do, I'm never getting this damn truck moving again, and we're walking."

"Let's not do that," Caleb replied. "Kilkenny, I'll lend you a clean pair of boxers if you shit your pants."

"I'm going to fuck you up the second we get there." Draven gripped the seat belt around his chest and gave it a hard tug, as if he was double-checking it was secure enough to hold him in place.

"Eww, nope. I have better taste than you."

"You're such a dick."

Their bickering, as annoying as it was, was the little piece of normal Kentucky needed to keep his focus where it should be—on the guardrails he could barely make out. "What are we down to?"

"Four miles."

"Thank fuck." He squinted his eyes, trying to see better. "This shit's getting worse."

"Yeah," Draven agreed. "But at least it's not a sandstorm and we aren't out there being cut to shreds."

"Truth."

Finally, Draven peered down at the GPS. "We're coming up on the turnoff. It's just after this next bend."

"Thank fuck."

"Not gonna disagree with you."

Kentucky shifted gears and tapped on the brakes repeatedly to slow them even further. But even that wasn't enough and instead of staying on the track, the truck ran straight over the snowbank which had built up near the tree line. "Shit."

"We almost made it." Caleb unclipped his belt and pushed at the door. "At least we aren't walking twenty freaking miles, so I'll take it."

"Me, too." Getting the door open wide enough to fit his big shoulders through the gap was a struggle. "I think I scraped off a couple of inches of muscles getting out."

"I didn't." Draven, the lucky bastard, had less snow at his side of the truck and was able to climb out easily, while Kentucky and Caleb were up to their knees in the snow. "At least it's not far from here."

"Yeah." He refused to be pissed about the truck. It had brought them here. They could pull it out of the ditch with the truck they'd left with Becky when the snow let up. "Let's go get warm." He jumped onto where he thought the path was and almost went sprawling when he landed on something buried in the snow. "Fuck."

"Did you hurt yourself, old man?"

"Caleb, I swear, I'm gonna add to my list again," he grumbled. "And I just swiped shit off it for you helping Becky feel better."

"No need to do that." Caleb dragged Kentucky forward until he was on the path. The snow still came up to their knees, but they could deal with the couple of minutes it would take to reach the cabins.

"I can't even see the lights from here. I hope the power is still on, as we didn't have time to show Becky where the generators are."

"It's still on," Draven said. "There, see? It's faint, but that's a light... right?"

Yes!

Relief flooded through him. They'd made it back and Becky wouldn't have to spend Christmas alone.

You either, he reminded himself.

Me either.

Through the window he could see the flickering of the TV. "Becky must still be up. The TV is on." He knocked at the door to warn her they were outside. "Becky, it's Kentucky, we're home," he called loudly and braced his hand on the door while he bent to unlace his boots.

"Tuck?"

"Yes, I have dumb and dumber with me, too." He figured letting her know it wasn't just him might be a good idea.

He heard the locks disengaging, but before he could shift his weight, the door opened, and he fell sideways into the house, knocking the breath out of himself.

"Eep. Crap!" Becky yelped. "Are you okay?" She dropped to her knees next to him. "I'm so sorry. I didn't know you were leaning against the door."

"Only my pride is bruised," he reassured her. "And that's only because those two are laughing their asses off at me." He smiled up at her and scrambled to his feet. "Let's get out of the way so we can shut the door on them."

"Shh, you." Becky swatted at his arm. "We can't do that. I don't know if they have enough brain cells between them to find the way to their own cabin. They'll freeze to death by morning."

"Hah." He tapped the tip of her nose. "I knew you were a smart one."

"I'll put on coffee."

The blush which darkened her cheeks he wanted to see that every freaking day of the week. "Thanks, I'd murder a cup."

"Are Caroline and RJ okay?" She moved across the room to the kitchen area and busied herself with the coffee pot. "How strong do you want this?"

"Strong, strong." He sat on a chair at the table to pull off his boots. "Both are fine, a little shook up. So is Rexar and Wolf."

"I'm so sorry that happened to them."

"Me, too." He hated when bad things happened to good people. "But they have a good support system and they'll be fine."

"Oh, good. I was so worried about them," she said. "I stress baked with the girls."

Kentucky sniffed the air. "I can smell it." He shucked off his coat and hung it on the hook on the back of the now closed door. "Did you have fun?"

"Yes. They are all so nice."

"I'm not sure I'd call Mamba nice," Draven muttered.

"You're only pissy that she said you can't be godfather to their baby," Becky shot back. She placed one mug under the coffee machine and hit start.

Kentucky snorted in laughter. "She's got you there, bro." He took the mug she handed him and scanned the room. "Did you find Jack in the shopping bags?"

"Yes." Becky pointed to the cupboard over the fridge. "It's up there. I opened the Baileys and spiked my hot chocolate earlier."

"Awesome." He pressed a kiss to the side of her head as he moved past her in his search for the bourbon.

"I hope you don't mind I had some, Caleb?"

"Not at all, that's what it's there for." He took the coffee she offered him and immediately held it out for Kentucky to add a splash of Jack to the mug.

"I'll put Baileys in mine." Draven dug into the pocket of his coat and came up with a spray bottle of whipped cream. "This bourbon caramel whipped cream will go awesome with it."

"Is that why you made us stop at Aldi on the way back?"

"Hell yes." Draven made a swirly top with the whipped cream on his coffee. "I was hoping they would have it. This stuff is better than any drug on the market. It's a good thing they only sell it at Christmastime, or I'd be as big as a bus."

"You kinda are."

He fucking loved that she was comfortable enough to tease his men. Loved. It. "You aren't mistaken." He wanted so badly to wrap his arms around her, but if she wasn't expecting it and it scared her, he'd kick his own ass. "You mentioned cookies?" His belly growled at the mention of food. Once they'd heard it had started snowing up here while Draven had been getting his whipped cream fix from the Aldi store, Kentucky hadn't dared take the time to stop for food, just in case they'd miss their window to get back.

"You're hungry." Becky had clearly heard his belly talking. Hell, he could still hear it talking. "Let me make you all some sandwiches and you can have some cookies."

"You don't need to cook for us, doll face…"

"Shoo, I want to." She waved her hands and pointed to the couch. "Go sit down. I'll make a full pot of coffee and you all watch TV or something."

"I'll help you."

"Nope." She pointed toward the couch. "Go wash your

hands, drink your coffee, and by the time you are done, I'll be ready."

It took a minute or two for him to read between the lines. While she was comfortable enough to tease and throw snark at them, she needed a little space to find her balance with so many men in the small cabin. He could give her that. "You heard my woman, boys. Clean up and sit down." He smacked at the hand Draven had snuck under a tea-towel, which covered what he hoped was the cookies. "Stop that. Wait until after your sandwiches."

"Damn, he's sounding more like my mom every freaking day."

"Pouting doesn't suit you." He shooed them down past the stairs and turned to wink at Becky when he saw she watched them. "Scrub under your nails, too," he ordered, just for shits and giggles.

"Tuck?"

"Yes?"

"Are any of you allergic to anything?"

"A-holes, Ma'am!" Caleb yelled from the bathroom before Kentucky could answer. "We're all allergic to a-holes."

"Noted!" Becky yelled back. "Sandwiches with no a-holes it is."

He pinched his eyes shut. "I can't freaking take them anywhere. I'm going to kill them." He smiled at her. "Did we buy any patience with the groceries?"

She placed some slices of bread on the counter and grabbed the mayonnaise from the fridge. "I think it's in the bottle called Jack Daniel's."

"Good thinking." He left the boys to their own devices and went back to add more to his mug. "Do you mind using butter on my sandwiches?" he asked. "And just make them with plain ham or chicken."

"Butter on sandwiches?"

"It's how my ma makes them for me." He lifted one shoulder and sipped on his coffee. "It's my favorite way to eat a sandwich."

"Then you've got it." She went back to the fridge for the butter. "It's a good thing I didn't use all the sticks when I was baking."

"Yeah, it sure is."

He watched her face as she put together the sandwiches. "How are you doing, baby?"

"I'm okay, now you are back."

"Good." Man, his heart did a weird little flop thing when she'd said that. "Do you need some help?"

"No, I promise." She smiled at him over her shoulder. "Your sandwich is ready. Have you washed your hands?" She quirked up one eyebrow at him.

"Umm."

"Off you go. Wash your hands."

She was laughing at him. He was sure that was what the sparkle in her eyes meant. And he loved it. "Gone." He hurried to do as she asked. Thankfully, the other two had vacated the bathroom and were now sitting on the couch, arguing over the remote. Just a normal family on Christmas Eve. Well, as normal as you could get when you lived in their world.

I want this. Not just on Christmas. But all the time.

He paused on the way back to grab the plate of sandwiches she offered him.

"Those are yours." She turned back to grab the other plate. "These are for the squabbling big kids."

"Great minds think alike." He gave the guys a warning look behind her back where she couldn't see. "I was just thinking that's what they're like." He decided he was going to sit at the table rather than in the vacant spot in between Caleb and Draven.

Becky grabbed a mug for herself and sat next to him. "Do you know the rest of that saying?" She watched him as he took a bite of the first sandwich, almost devouring half of it with one bite.

He munched fast so he wouldn't have to speak with his mouth full. "Huh?" She made a damn good sandwich. It was as good as his ma would make.

"Great minds think alike. Do you know the rest of it?"

He sipped his coffee to wash down the food. "There's more?"

"Yes." She nodded. "Great minds think alike, but fools seldom differ."

"The fools are behind us." He planned on ignoring them if he could. "And it's true they seldom differ." He lowered his voice to a whisper, as if he was sharing a massive secret. "If one of them screws up, you can be sure the other is helping him do it." He nudged the plate toward her. "Want to try one with butter?"

"Oh, yes, please." She took a triangle and sniffed at it before nibbling on the center, away from the crust. He watched the expressions crossing her face as she tasted, then took another bite. "It's different. Good, but different." She got to her feet. "It needs some mustard though. I'll be back."

"Sure."

She came back with the mustard and a butter knife. Opening what remained of her sandwich, she slathered it with mustard and closed it again before taking a bite. "Oh my God, this is good. Here, taste." She held it out to him, and there wasn't a chance on the planet he was going to say no.

His mouth skimmed off her fingers as he took a bite. Flavor burst over his tongue. Not from the sandwich, awesome as it was, it was that taste of her which made him groan.

"Are you two making love to the foo—ow—what was that

for?" Caleb yelped. Kentucky didn't need to look over his shoulder to know Draven had smacked him.

"Because you're a dumbass," Draven muttered. "Which means I get to pick the movie."

He ignored the guys in favor of Becky. "You're right, it's awesome with mustard." She didn't have to know there might be a double meaning behind his words. And when she put her stockinged feet on the rung of his chair, he figured it had gone right over her head.

"What about *Elf*?" Draven asked. "Or *The Polar Express*?"

"I don't mind." Becky wiped her hands with a napkin from the holder in the middle of the table. "I haven't seen either of them, so you guys can pick if you have a favorite."

"They are going to have to draw lots," Kentucky told her. "Just watch and see."

"Have they seen them?"

"They've seen the *Elf* one. One year when we were in Afghanistan, over Christmas, they watched it about seventy billion times."

Driving me batshit with it.

But there was no way he was saying that out loud. He was just hoping they'd pick the other one.

"What are they about?" She leaned forward and grabbed his arm as she peered around him at the guys. "Gimme a rundown and I'll help you choose."

He tuned out the conversation to watch her as she paid attention to both of them. He lowered his face until his nose was almost touching her hair and sniffed. How in the hell did she smell of strawberries? He didn't remember buying strawberry shampoo. But wow. He made a mental note to remember to buy some everyday in the future.

"I think *The Polar Express*." She leaned back and winked at him where the guys couldn't see. "Whatcha think?"

"Sounds good to me." The little minx had been making

sure he wasn't tortured by *Elf* again. "I love you. I fucking love you for doing this," he whispered softly.

"You're welcome."

She might never know that he meant the words just as they were. He loved her. He loved everything about her. She just didn't know it. He hid his nose behind his coffee mug to keep her from catching a glimpse of his face, because he wasn't entirely confident he could keep the truth concealed by will power alone.

"Cookies, anyone?" Becky got to her feet. "Tuck, can you pull a chair in front of the couch so I can put a plate on it? It means we won't have to keep getting up to grab more cookies."

"Of course."

"Thank you." She turned away and climbed the stairs. "I'll be back in a sec. Don't start without me."

"She's bossy."

"Yup, Draven, she totally is."

"And you love it." Draven lowered his voice so it wouldn't carry.

Kentucky grinned at his teammates. "Yeah, I totally do." He didn't care if they gave him shit for it. It—no, she—was worth a little mudslinging. He glimpsed movement over his head out of the corner of his eye and ducked, rolling out of the way when a beanbag landed next to him.

"Um—" Becky leaned over the railing of the loft, amusement all over her face. "Watch out?"

"You almost hit me on the head."

"You big baby, it's a beanbag. Unless you want to be sitting on the bare floor." She smirked at him. "Or you can sit on the beanbag…" she glanced at the others, then back to him, "and I sit there with you."

He nodded in answer because words failed him. If she was sitting next to him, she could thump him on the head with fifty freaking bags filled with little white balls and he wouldn't whine, bitch, or complain about it. He went to grab some glasses from the cupboard so he could shift the front of his pants around to make some more room without her seeing. Although from the snickers from the peanut gallery on the couch, neither Draven nor Caleb had missed it.

By the time the intro music was playing, his back was to the center seat of the couch, with Becky hovering over him. He waited for her to decide how and where she wanted to sit, and did an internal fist pump when she nudged his foot with hers. When he widened his knees, she sat between them and rested her head against him.

"Is this okay?"

"Perfect." He nuzzled the side of her head. "Shh, now, relax and watch the movie."

"Yeah." She took his glass of Jack, sipped from it, and handed it back to him. A shudder ran through her, which he felt all the way to his bones.

How the hell did I get this damn lucky?

Don't question it, dude. Enjoy this time with her.

CHAPTER NINETEEN

Becky's eyes blinked open, and she stared at the wooden boards above her. She stiffened when she didn't recognize them.

Where am I?

Think.

Think.

"Boss, we're leaving," a voice whispered from somewhere. She knew that voice, she was sure of it. But right this second, with panic swirling through her, she couldn't place it. "We'll be back soon."

"Mmmh-kay. Make sure the door is locked behind you."

"Wh—what?" She scrambled away from the voice with her fists balled up, ready to lash out at whoever that was. Both fight and flight had kicked in with a vengeance.

"If you're going to punch me, can you do it fast and knock me out? My head is thumping, and I'd appreciate it if you put me out of my misery."

She blinked at the shape she could barely make out in the dark. What on earth was she doing in bed with him? Had she blanked everything out again? Nope, that didn't feel right.

She swallowed down the panic and forced herself to try and remember.

"You fell asleep watching the movie. I carried you up here and couldn't leave unless I left you my shirt, as your hands were wrapped up in it."

Tuck. That's Tuck.

Relief knocked the wind out of her.

Tuck will never hurt me.

"I'm sorry," she said in a small voice as mortification set in. She'd bolted away from him as if he had the plague.

"S'ok, doll face." Kentucky's voice was husky with sleep. "Come, lay back down. We have a few hours before we need to start cooking that dinner you planned last night."

"Last night me was an idiot." Now that she recognized him, her heartbeat slowed from the galloping thing it had going on to a slow trot, but she figured that was the best she could do at this point. "What was I thinking?"

"That it's Christmas, and you persuaded Draven Kilkenny that he was on vegetable peeling duties." He reached a hand toward her, almost touching but not quite, and turned his hand over, palm up. "Will you sleep with me some more?" he asked. "Please."

How a man with muscles which went on for days could be so fricking gentle was beyond her. She placed her hand in his and used it to give herself leverage to scoot across the bed until she was next to him. "Yes."

"Thank you." He pushed one arm under her head and wrapped the other around her waist. "If you want to get free, just say the word," he said sleepily. "I swear I'll let you go."

"I will."

"Good girl." He kissed the top of her head. "Merry Christmas, doll face."

"Merry Christmas." She allowed herself to fade into his chest, soaking in the closeness. This was something she'd thought would never be possible for her again. But right here, right now, she'd take it for the gift it was. "Sleepy."

"Me, too."

It didn't take long for Kentucky's breathing to even out again, and she just enjoyed the peace of laying here with him wrapped around her, fast asleep. She smoothed her hand over his chest. He didn't deserve to be stuck with her. She was broken. He needed better than she was. Maybe the best Christmas gift she could give him was to disappear. But… and it was a big but…

Lawd, the way he's breathing me in. HELP. I'm never going to be able to convince myself that I can walk away from him.

She lifted her face to press a kiss to the side of his throat and internally fanned herself at the sexy, growly noise he made in his sleep. That noise should be illegal. He shouldn't be able to make that noise. If she were wearing panties, they'd just poof and disappear right out from under the sweatpants, which doubled as jammies. But holy heck, that noise was addictive. She pressed another small kiss to his skin and reveled in the feminine power which swept through her. She knew most of what she told herself was absolute lies because their connection was undeniable.

I'm so screwed.

And so is he if…

"Don't stop, doll face, I love your mouth on me."

So here we go!

But she shook off the memories which probed at the edges of her mind. As if outside herself in the dim light thrown by the night light, she could just about make out the shape of her fingers as they moved against his skin.

Look at those nervous hands.

In her head, she counted to three and lifted her lowered eyelids to peer up at him. She was so far out of her comfort zone, it wasn't funny.

His reaction was so cute and melted some of the fear inside her. He just said, "Wow."

Talk about making a girl feel good.

"Can I have a hug?"

A little confused that he wasn't taking over and instead was allowing her to lead, she obliged him and wrapped her arms around his back, squeezing tightly. She almost wished they had a mirror, so she could see how good they looked together. *Almost.*

You don't need a mirror to see how you fit in his arms. Can you not feel the chemistry? Oh boy, get out that internal fan... because, sister, I have a feeling we are going to need it.

He shifted around on the bed, taking her with him until he lay against the pillows with her straddling his waist. For long seconds, they stared at each other. She wasn't even sure if they were breathing. But he waited for her to find her balance. When she stroked one finger down across the dimple which was almost hidden in his short beard, he did not disappoint her. His hand swiped the hair out of her face, and he turned that dimpled smile of his to level megawatt, almost to the point where she could feel the heat of it brushing her skin.

Holy cow.

"You lead, babe." Kentucky ran his hand up her leg from her knee to mid-thigh. "I will follow you."

Oh, that's... wow... hot.

She could feel it in both their body language when they started to get more comfortable with each other, and she felt the tension drain from her shoulders. His hands were warm on her legs as he petted and soothed the anxiety she needed to keep from taking over until she reached the point where she was comfortable enough that she leaned down to press a kiss to his mouth. She moved her mouth across his, the bristles of his beard rubbing against her skin, adding an extra level of... hotness... to the sensations. She could feel when his need to take over came dangerously close to breaking his self-control and she pulled back. "I promise I'm okay."

Going...

Going...

She watched the expressions cross his face so fast she couldn't figure out what they were.

"Are you sure?"

"Yes."

Gone!

She didn't even breathe as he reached up and tugged her down to his mouth. When he kissed her, it was stunningly beautiful in its simplicity and called to everything which ached inside her. Both struggled to catch their breath when the need for air ended the kiss.

"I know I keep saying it." Kentucky tucked her hair behind her ears. "But wow. Do you have any idea what you are doing to me here?"

"I can hazard a guess based on what's underneath me." She gave a little experimental wriggle of her hips. Instead of the pain she'd expected, her lady parts decided they remembered how things worked and fired to life with a vengeance.

"I'm so screwed."

She shook her head. "No... that's later."

"Minx." He pressed a kiss to her cheek. "Do you have any idea how amazing you look?" Another kiss, this one hot near her ear. "You are a lioness, and don't you forget it."

"Rawr." She couldn't help herself—the word burst out of her mouth on a giggle, and he flashed her that dimpled smile of his again. "How come this dimple doesn't show all the time?" She ran her finger down his face and into his beard.

"I have a dimple—are you sure?"

He had to be teasing her. "Yes, you do. Right here." She leaned over him and kissed him just over it.

"I'm not sure I believe you." He tilted his head to one side, giving her more access. "Maybe you should do that again. You know, just to be sure it's really there."

They both stared at each other and both nervously giggled as if they weren't exactly sure why this heat which flared between them didn't just burn, but it teased and climbed slowly. If she had to admit anything to herself, it was hearing Kentucky Smith giggle as he lay under her was not only hot as sin, but it was totally and utterly adorable. He couldn't take his eyes off of her and she loved it.

Was every woman on the planet blind? Did they not see how freaking amazing this man was?

You didn't see him either. He meant protection... when did that become more?

She wasn't sure when things had changed between them for her. And as more kisses happened between them, she didn't care, and she didn't think he did either, as she could feel that he was as happy to be here with her as she was with him. This, them together, just felt so natural.

"My cheeks hurt from smiling." Kentucky winked at her with a saucy smirk on his face. "Maybe you could kiss them better."

"Oh, they do? We wouldn't want that to happen." She did as he asked and skimmed her lips over his cheeks, laying butterfly wing soft kisses on him until his hand skimmed up her body to her face. "Love when you do that," she admitted softly.

"Do what, my gorgeous lioness queen?"

"When you stroke my face with your thumb. Just like that." She leaned into his hand, rubbing her cheek into his palm. Her breath caught in her throat when his hand moved to her neck to pull her in for another kiss.

SOS. Send the fire brigade. This cabin is gonna burn despite all the snow on the ground. Send water. Turn on a fan. The man could bring a corpse back to life with a kiss like that.

He wrapped his hand around the side of her neck and tilted her head with his thumb under her chin. She opened her mouth for him and his tongue swept inside in an all-consuming kiss.

Becky wondered if he liked that hand on the neck thing as much as she did. She pressed against him and snaked her hand up his side, making him shiver, then wrapped her fingers around his throat with her palm pressed gently against his Adam's apple. She smiled against his mouth, because if the growl which rumbled up from his chest was anything to go by, he was here for it and loving her hand on his throat. She made a mental note to remember to do it again, because that growl was everything.

His free hand moved up and down her thigh, then wrapped around her waist. Everything which had held her back before disappeared from the room and she wasn't one bit mad about it. Because how he made her feel and the desire which made her crave more was almost too much to bear, but she wouldn't change what was happening between them for anything. She needed to have him guide her forward with murmurs, growls, and groans. But she also loved that he drank in her sighs and moans and encouraged her to give him more, with a touch of his fingertips here and a kiss there.

He shifted them on the bed so he was sitting more upright and her knees lay on the bed at either side of his hips. He kept one hand flat on the small of her back and kissed her until she forgot how breathing worked.

"Fire. I'm definitely on fire."

"I fucking love it." He pressed a kiss to the center of her throat. "Let me show my queen of a woman how much I appreciate every inch of her." She leaned her head back on her shoulders as he tugged the collar of her t-shirt aside to expose one shoulder. Everywhere he could touch, he touched. If his lips could reach it, they kissed it. She couldn't deny it, they just fit together so well. They cuddled like they'd been doing it for a lifetime, as if this connection between them was soul bound.

When he reached for her hand, turned it over, and pressed a kiss to her palm, she was done. If she was the one laying against the sheets, she'd have melted into them. Instead, she sank against his chest. She needed more… wanted more…

"Never tell anyone that I had you almost naked in my lap," he whispered against her ear, "and that I didn't make love to you. They'll think I wasn't able to get it up."

She stared at him for a minute, trying to make sense of the words, when a giggle bubbled up inside her. In seconds, he joined her, and they giggled together like a pair of teenagers. His words had taken the pressure she hadn't known was there off, and now they could just be. The more he just kissed, explored, and worshipped her, the more she did the same to him. She knew better than anyone that sex was often just that: sex. But this—this was so hot, so sweet—and so much more. At this point, it was like they had been together forever.

She turned around, putting her back to his chest, and he placed a kiss first on the right side of her neck, and then on the left. She intertwined her fingers with his and lifted his hand to place it at her throat while dropping her head back on his shoulder. "Tuck." She sighed when he planted kisses just under her ear. She glanced at him out of the corner of her eye. Rugged men weren't supposed to be beautiful. But to her, he was just that. A beautiful man, a wonderful person, and hot enough that when he sweetly kissed her cheek while his hand was on her throat, it was heart achingly beautiful.

As they lay there together kissing and learning about each other, it was like they were already creating small secrets together and she never wanted it to stop. But as always, just when she had found her happy place, life came calling in the form of a solid knock on the door.

"Hey, Kentucky, Becky!" Caleb yelled. "Are y'all up? It's time to cook."

"Is murder reeealllly wrong?" She didn't want this time between them to stop. "Maybe we can ignore them. You told them to lock the door when they left earlier."

"They'll just pick the locks." He kissed her cheek once again. "Come on. Up you get. We'll do Christmas, then revisit… us."

Lawd, didn't that send a shiver down her spine. "I still think murder should be a possibility for their untimely interruption."

"I agree." He helped her off the bed and got to his feet. Lowering his head until his mouth was right next to her ear, he whispered, "Just think how much better it will be after all the anticipation of waiting."

"Damn." Maybe it was him she should murder in his sleep. But it would be a damn shame to do so. The world would be a lot worse off without Kentucky Smith to grace it with his presence. She glared over the railing at the front door when the guys pounded on it again. "Go let them in before they break it down. I'm going to jump in the shower."

"Yes, Ma'am."

CHAPTER TWENTY

Kentucky put his hand on the oven and glanced at his watch. It had to be time to check the roasting ham by now. They'd all agreed turkey wasn't their jam, so they were having ham with all the fixings. His belly had been growling for two freaking hours, teased by all the aromas and smells which filled the entire cabin.

"If you open that oven," Becky called, "I swear you won't get any cheesecake."

He glanced at the stairs and frowned when he didn't see her. How the heck had she known what he'd been about to do? "It smells done."

"It needs at least another hour, or maybe hour and a half, before we pull it out and rest it. Finish peeling the potatoes for the mash."

For someone who was normally pretty darn good with a blade, he'd cut his fingers three times already. The cabin didn't have enough sharp knives to go around, so he'd opted to use his K-bar for peeling, which, not that he'd ever admit it, hadn't been the most intelligent option on the planet. "Damn it."

"I heard that."

Grumbling under his breath, he went back to the sink and picked up another potato. "What are you doing up there?"

"Mind your business. You'll find out soon."

"Dude, she's slinging out orders like it's going out of style," Caleb whispered next to him, chopping carrots. "Do you think she picked it up from the other women when they were baking? Because if so, in my opinion the women folk at the ranch are a bad influence."

"I keep saying that," Draven said. "But nobody listens to me."

"That's because you do shit by trial and error." Kentucky had exactly zero qualms about telling Draven how it was. "Mostly error."

"Like, a shit ton of error." Caleb never had been one to pass up an opportunity to throw down some shit talking and teasing.

"Tuck, can you grab this for me?"

Saved by Becky's voice before the other two decided to start throwing some teasing about Becky his way, and thereby preventing murder at Christmas, he dropped the blade on the countertop and pulled the plug on the sink. "Coming." There had to be enough potatoes peeled at this point. There were only freaking four of them. "Why didn't we buy the peel and vacuum sealed potatoes again?"

"Because they cost enough to feed a small country and it only takes five minutes to wash and peel the normal ones ourselves."

Five minutes? My ass, was that five minutes? I've been doing that shit for at least an hour.

He paused at the top of the stairs, his eyes widening at the chaos strewn across their bed. "What's going on?"

Becky knotted the string she had in her hand and tugged, revealing a long rope of something. "Popcorn garlands. The tree needs to be decorated some more, and we didn't have time to do it last night because we got stuck in the movie and then I fell asleep."

Yes, she had fallen asleep, and she'd done it all over him. There wasn't a chance in hell he was going to make her feel bad about it. Because he really hoped that wasn't a one and done event. "That's what you have been doing up here?"

"Yes, we didn't know we'd have a tree that size, so I didn't get enough stuff for it at the store."

Did she not know that a decorated tree wasn't what was important here? Important was she was here with him and he with her. The two idiots downstairs didn't count, in his opinion. This was his and Becky's first Christmas together. He didn't want her stressing over a tree. "You know we could decorate the side we look at and nobody would notice... right?"

"Yeah, but where is the fun in that?" She handed him an armful of popcorn strings. "If you aren't done with the potatoes, ask either Draven or Caleb to put those on the tree for me, please. I'll be down in a minute. I just want to finish this last one."

"You got it, doll face, I'm done. We have enough potatoes to feed that small country you were talking about." He caught an escapee garland and tucked it under his chin. "You need anything else?"

"Just a clear spot on the floor to make some paper baubles, if that's okay."

He absolutely loved how adorable she was as she grinned up at him from the bed. "Paper baubles. If you want help, then Draven is your guy. He's always making stuff out of paper."

"Perfect." She scrambled off the bed and hugged him, nearly giving the garlands an escape route. "As soon as he's done slicing the sprouts, he can help me make some out of that card paper we got."

He nodded and left her to it. Not one of them had thought about presents. Just being together was enough this year. But if his Becky wanted popcorn all over the tree, then he was wrapping popcorn strings all around the tree until there were no more popcorn strings for him to wrap.

Draven scraped what looked like the last of his Brussels sprouts into a pot. "Whatcha got, Ken?"

"Popcorn for the tree." He dumped them on the floor. "Becky will need a hand with some paper shit in a minute."

"Umm, what paperwork is so important it has to be done on Christmas?"

Trust Draven to be all kinds of confused about it. "Baubles." Kentucky stood back and glanced at the potted tree. He switched on the lights to help him see where the gaps in the decorations were better and picked up the end of the first string. How hard could it be to wrap them around it? "Paper baubles."

"Awesome." Draven brought the pot to the stove top and yelled up the stairs. "Becky?"

"Yes?"

"Do I need to put the sprouts on?"

"Nope, not for about ten more minutes," she replied. "I'll be down in two seconds with some paper."

"Okay." Draven went to the drawers and checked in the first two before asking over his shoulder, "Do we have scissors?"

"I have both the pairs we found in the drawers here." Becky checked the stairs to see where her foot would land on the top step, then carefully made her way down the stairs. "I was using them for the garlands." She dropped the paper, tinsel, and all the other bits and pieces on the couch, then sat cross-legged on the floor beside it. "We may need to replace them, because it's rude to ruin their scissors by cutting paper and not doing so."

"I'll take care of it." Kentucky pulled out his notebook and scribbled it down to remind himself to fix it for her as soon as he was able.

"What kind of baubles do you want?" Draven sat near Becky and grabbed a handful of red and white paper.

"I don't mind." She started folding some gold sparkled paper. "I'll make a star for the top, because we forgot that, too." She smiled across the room at him. "Will you put on the potatoes in five minutes? And then you can help Draven with this and I'll make sure everything is ready for dinner. Or do you prefer to do the cooking?"

He wasn't entirely sure if he knew how to make baubles, but he would give it a go just because she asked it of him. "I'll take baubles, unless you want a dinner which dogs in about three counties would turn up their noses at."

"Please don't let him cook," Caleb begged. "Last time he made grilled cheese, it was blacker than the truck, and he put veggies in it."

"Ew." Becky shuddered. "Veggies do not belong in grilled cheese."

"Told ya, Ken, only heathens put veggies in grilled cheese." Caleb put his carrots on the stove. "Will I turn them on for you, Miss Becky?"

The fucker was being all kinds of polite so he wouldn't be conscripted into making decorations.

"Yes, please." Becky kept her concentration on the paper and scissors she was using. "Just please make sure there is at least a half pot of water in each and turn them on high. When they boil, Kentucky can take over here and you can help me with the table, if that works?"

"Deal." Caleb immediately started lifting lids off pots and

checking them before turning on the stove rings under each one. "Setting the table is something I can do."

Kentucky surveyed his efforts with the garland and turned to go help Draven when the sound of his phone ringing had him changing direction to where it danced across the counter near the fridge. He glanced at the screen and answered the call. "Hey, Ma, Merry Christmas." She never failed. Every single year since he'd left for boot camp at midday on Christmas Day, she called him. Even when he was home, because she didn't want to break what had become their tradition.

"Merry Christmas, Ken. I love you."

"I love you, too, Ma. Are you all set for dinner?" He winked at Becky and went to sit in the only available spot, the stairs. "Who's there with you this year?"

"I'm having dinner with Susan and her husband Pat, and Kevin, too." His ma loved Christmas and feeding people was certainly her thing. "Oh, and we have Johnson. Do you remember him?"

"Dad's friend from Teams?"

"Yes, he stopped in to see us on his way to Idaho," Ma said. "He has nobody left at home, so he was just going to drive through last night and get home. I know what you men are like. He'd have had pot noodle or something."

"How's he doing?"

"Good as can be expected when you get to our age." His mother did like to tell everyone she was old and feeble, yet let a fight break out at the bar and she would wade into the middle with no concern for her age or feebleness.

"So rocking it and thinking he's half his age?"

"Yes. Are you working? Do you have time to at least eat some dinner today?"

"I'm not working, and my Becky is putting the finishing touches on dinn—"

"Whoa, whoa, whoa."

Crap. He hadn't meant to tell her like this. He made eye contact with his Becky where she stood at the stove with a potholder in her hands and her eyes wide in her beautiful face, and winked at her.

"You have a Becky?"

He yanked the phone away from his ear when his mother screeched loudly at him.

"Becky is such a lovely name.

"Is she as lovely as her name, Ken?

"What am I saying? Of course she is.

"When are you bringing her home to meet me?

"Son?

"Ken?

"Are you not answering me?"

"Because you are talking a mile a minute and I can't get a word in edgewise?" Now the shock of letting it slip to his mother that Becky was in his life... he decided it wasn't a bad thing after all. He wanted his mother to know she was a part of his life. "She's lovely, my Becky. You'll love her." He blew out a slow breath. "And she's mine as long as she'll keep me."

"Oh..."

Shit, was his ma crying?

"You sound just like your father."

"Ah." He wasn't entirely sure what he should say to that. His father hadn't always been the best husband. He'd been more married to the Navy than he had been to his family. But he'd tried. Kentucky would give him that. The man had definitely tried.

Becky crossed the kitchen and handed him a mug. "It's coffee. Go sit on the porch and visit with your momma." She ran her fingers over his hair. "I've got this, I promise."

"Oh, she sounds so lovely." His ma sighed in his ear. "Can I talk to her?"

Given the terror which crept into Becky's eyes, he was guessing she heard the request, too. "Not this time, Ma, but soon. I promise."

"Okay."

"Shoo, out of my kitchen," Becky whispered. "Go visit with your momma."

He hesitated as he wasn't entirely sure the other two could be trusted not to act like a pair of toddlers if they found the adult supervision had left the room.

"I promise, I'll chase them with a wooden spoon if they step out of line," Becky promised in a low whisper.

Obviously, it wasn't low enough as his ma hummed in his ear, "She sounds like me when you and the two hooligans you call friends were young."

He pulled the phone away from his ear. "Are you sure?"

"Yes." Becky nodded and leaned up.

He just knew that kiss was aimed for his cheek, but he turned his head and stole one straight from her lips instead. Now, she had a reason to have wide eyes. "If you're sure."

"Go, go." She waved him off. "Merry Christmas, Mrs. Smith." She spoke loud enough that his mother could hear.

"Merry Christmas, child."

"She says Merry Christmas back." He stepped over Draven's legs on the way to the door. It didn't take a rocket scientist to figure out his mother was going to grill him with rapid-fire questions faster than a senior chief on the grinder. But he'd take it all with a smile on his face. His ma was just happy for him and he wasn't one bit averse to bragging to her about his Becky.

CHAPTER TWENTY-ONE

"I'm stuffed. I don't think I could eat another bite." Becky patted her belly. Thankfully, she was wearing stretchy pants. If she'd been wearing jeans, she'd have had to pop the button on them for sure.

"There's still cheesecake, right?"

"How in the name of anything can you even consider eating more right now, Tuck?" She surveyed the table. Everything was down to scraps except for the ham. They should be able to get at least a sandwich from that later tonight or tomorrow. "You guys are hounds."

"We're growing boys." Draven munched on a stray carrot, which had dropped over the edge of his plate. "The food was yummy. Thank you for cooking."

"You're welcome."

"We're clearing up." Kentucky pinned the guys with a stare, as if daring them to contradict him. "You cooked."

"Um, we all cooked." She patted his arm. He was very sweet to want to do it, and if she'd been responsible for the entire meal, she'd have taken him up on it in a heartbeat. "It will only take a couple of minutes if we all pitch in."

Thankfully, nobody argued, but got to their feet and started loading the dishwasher with everything they'd used to make dinner.

Becky grabbed a pot lid from the sink, and when she turned, something on the tree caught her attention as it just looked off. She handed the lid to Kentucky and went to investigate. Out of the corner of her eye, she could see Draven's smirk.

That little shit did something to our tree.

Draven had been tasked with finishing the paper baubles by himself, therefore she concentrated on the food. She touched the first few, which were beautifully folded and bauble shaped. But her hand stilled when she reached for a red one.

I'm going to kill him.

"Draven?"

"Yes, Ma'am?"

Oh, he wants to play innocent, does he?

"Can you tell me what kind of bauble this is?" She was going to make him say it out—freaking—loud.

"A tally-whacker one, Ma'am."

Please don't blush.

Please do not let me blush right now.

She slapped what she hoped was a stern look on her face and turned with the paper tally-whacker bauble, as Draven called it, in her hand. She glanced down and realized how exactly she was holding it and changed her grip on it so she wasn't holding the dick-shaped paper bauble by the shaft. "And what exactly is it doing?"

Kentucky choked and smacked Caleb on the arm, clearly telling him to shut his trap and not get involved. Smart man, because she was going to have to get freaking creative on her payback.

"Umm..."

"What is it doing, Draven?" Never mind a mom voice, she wasn't equipped with one of those, but kindergarten teacher voice… that one she had down pat and used it to her advantage.

"I believe it's arriving, Ma'am?"

Arriving my butt, that's not what I'd call arriving.

"Are you asking or telling me?"

Oh, look at him squirming.

But she didn't dare show her amusement. He'd never learn a lesson if she didn't make him squirm a little bit more. Draven Kilkenny, she decided, was going to drive some poor woman demented at some point.

I better start stocking up on wine and popcorn, because when that woman puts him in his place, it is going to be epic.

"Am…"

"Asking or telling, Draven? It's a simple question." Let the little shit squirm some more. He could glance at Kentucky for direction all he wanted. But he better not be getting any from her man, because if Kentucky knew what was good for him, he'd stay well out of this situation.

"Telling." He scrubbed his hand down over his face.

"And what's it doing?" she prompted him, just as she would have one of her students.

"Coming, Ma'am."

Was she the only one in the room who noticed he'd switched to calling her Ma'am the second he'd realized he'd been caught in his mischief making? "Why, pray tell, is there a paper tally-whacker coming all over my Christmas tree?" She knew it wasn't really her tree, but she figured that was just Semantics at this stage.

"Becau—" Draven stuttered, but continued because Kentucky nudged him with his boot, probably where he thought she couldn't see. "Because I thought it was funny."

Inspiration struck, and she turned and hung the bauble back on the tree and beckoned to him. "Come with me."

"Huh?"

"Do as my lady asks," Kentucky growled.

Thank you for backing me up.

She thanked him silently with a smile as she tugged on her coat. "Don't think I don't see you grabbing those beers out of the fridge, Caleb."

"Is it okay to bring them?" Caleb's head popped around the fridge door.

Hadn't she just made a mental note to buy herself wine for just such an occasion a little while ago? "Of course it is."

"Yes." Caleb handed a bottle to Kentucky and one for himself. "Do you want one, too, Becks?"

"No, thank you. I'm going to need my hands free for a bit."

"What are you up to?"

Kentucky's whisper in her ear sent a shiver of awareness down her spine. She glanced around to make sure Draven wasn't in earshot before she whispered back, "Snow angels."

"You aren't mad?"

"Only that he didn't tell me what he was doing, so I could do some, too."

"I fucking love you." Kentucky placed his hand on the small of her back and urged her through the door. "Give him hell, baby."

There he was doing it again. Saying he loved her. This had to be just his way. She refused to allow herself to read too much into it. "I plan to."

"Awesome." Kentucky swiped the snow off one chair on the porch and sat down. Caleb followed his lead. Clearly, both men were staying out of the line of fire. Although Kentucky knew she hadn't evil planned for his teammate, he wasn't stopping her from having a little fun at Draven's expense either.

"Drop and give me twenty," she ordered in her best teacher voice. She quirked up an eyebrow when Draven glanced at Kentucky before heaving out a sigh and shucking off his jacket. She totally knew he didn't understand what she meant. Maybe it was a little bit mean of her. She held back a giggle by pure force of will when he dropped into the snow, as if he was going to do push-ups. "Nuh—uh." She tugged on the back of his shirt. "Flip over, you're making snow angels."

"What?"

"Not push-ups, Draven. Snow angels." She couldn't stop the giggles escaping this time, even when she covered her mouth with her hand.

"I'm traumatized enough with push-ups," Draven grumbled, but good-naturedly did as she asked and flipped over onto his back.

She picked up his coat and held it out to him. "Put this on before you catch your death."

"You aren't mad?"

Bless him, he was all kinds of confused.

"Only that you didn't tell me, so we could make more and drive the other two insane by trying to figure out what was wrong with the tree," she replied.

He took the coat and put it on. "Ya knows, you'd make an awesome sister, right?"

Sister? It had been a long time since she had someone to call family. A girl could do a hell of a lot worse than to call Draven Kilkenny brother. "Are you adopting me?"

Now that his coat was back on, he flopped over onto his back and started making the snow angels. "Does it mean I get to give Ken shit if he messes you about?"

"Absolutely."

"Deal."

Somehow she'd managed to find herself a brother for Christmas. When Draven came close to kicking her as he did his snow angel duty, she stepped a little further away from him, but closer to the cabin.

"The last time I had this much fun at Christmas was when his father was alive and brought home some of the strays from his team to spend the holidays with them." She heard Kentucky say as he watched her standing over Draven as he lay in the snow, moving his hands and legs. "I never thought I'd see that in my lifetime."

"Me either." Caleb tapped his bottle off Kentucky's. "Your woman is mean. I don't want to get on the wrong side of her."

"My woman is not mean, and if it didn't mean moving my butt off this comfy chair, I'd punch you just for shits and giggles. She's a fucking lioness."

I shouldn't be eavesdropping, but OMG.

She had no idea why Kentucky thought she was strong enough to be a lioness, but it was way better than a mouse in her opinion, so she'd take it.

"Lionesses can be mean."

"Only when they are protecting what's important."

Out of the corner of her eye, she saw Kentucky sipping on his beer. It was a crying shame that his coat was buttoned up tight and she couldn't see how his Adam's apple bobbed up and down when he swallowed.

"And the tree is what was important today?"

"I don't quite understand it either, because I think the dick baubles are fucking hilarious. But if it's important to Becky, then it's important, period." Kentucky sipped from his beer bottle again, then cupped his hand around his mouth. "You make for a fine snow angel, Kilkenny."

"Fuck you, Ken, just fuck you."

"Serves you right for being a dick."

"I wasn't being a dick!" Draven yelled back. "Please tell me we get to pelt them with snowballs."

She stared at Draven for a second. "A snowball fight?"

"Oh, sister dearest, I'm talking a snowball ambush rather than a fight. A fight suggests they are aware it's coming."

She thought about it for a second, then nodded. "I like the way you think. Keep making angels, I'm going to make us up a bunch of snowballs."

"But they'll see you doing it," Draven whispered. "That defeats the purpose of an ambush."

"Nope." She glanced over her shoulder at the other two men on the porch. "They're gonna think I'm going to pelt you with the snowballs. It won't occur to them that we have joined forces against them."

"And they say men are the deadly species, hah." Draven snorted. "Get to making them, my ass is getting cold."

She giggled manically as she made a bunch of snowballs. Maybe doing this chosen family thing wouldn't be so bad after all.

CHAPTER TWENTY-TWO

"Ken, she's making snowballs." Caleb moved his chair a little, clearly wanting a better view of what was happening below them. "Do you think she's going to pelt him?"

"Looks like it." Should he be worried? Was this getting a little out of hand? "Make sure you don't put rocks in the snowballs," he called. He didn't know if she'd been around much snow before.

"Hell, no." Caleb smacked him on the arm. "Don't tell her that. Let her smack him with the rock-filled freeze-balls."

"Snowballs," Kentucky corrected.

"I think freeze-balls sounds better," Caleb shot back. "Because Kilkenny is going to be freezing his balls off by the time she's—oopf."

He stared in shock at the snowball which had hit Caleb straight in the face and burst out laughing. "Oh, fuck, that shit's funn—"

Splat.

Cold exploded all over his face. He stared at Becky in shock, not quite understanding what was happening. She pulled back her arm and let another snowball fly. Kentucky ducked, and the snowball landed on the side of Caleb's head.

"Shit."

He and Caleb glanced at each other and nodded. "Snowball fight."

"Yes!"

They bounded over the small railing surrounding the porch and swiftly called up some snow, all the while being pelted with balls from the other two.

"When the heck did they join forces?" Caleb, the asshole, ducked in behind him so he wasn't directly in the line of fire. "I thought he was the one going to be..." He jumped when Kentucky ducked and he got hit again. "Asshole, stop doing that."

"I don't know, damn it." He also didn't care. If pelting them with snowballs made Becky laugh like that, then he was all for it. If only he could figure out a way to avoid being the one with a target. He grabbed Caleb by the shoulders and dragged him around in front of him. "You're a human shield."

"Fuck you." Caleb struggled and kicked against him, trying to get free. "Ken, you're an asshole."

"Yup." He grinned at Becky over Caleb's head, then ducked again when Draven this time, let fly with his cold weapon.

Kentucky practically threw Caleb over the bank of snow which lay between their cabin and the next one, giving them as much cover as possible. "Weapon up, bro, because payback is going to be epic." His hands were already balling up snow. He exposed himself enough to lamp one snowball toward Draven and ducked back into cover before he could get another one in the face.

"Hooyah!" Caleb yelled the battle cry as he, too, sent snowballs sailing over their scant cover. "Take that, suckers."

They could hear Becky and Draven running in the snow,

but it was almost impossible to tell which one of them was going where. "They're splitting up."

"Yeah, I hear them." Caleb placed another snowball into the stack, which was rapidly growing between them. "Where the hell are they?"

"If it was me." Kentucky lay flat on his chest as he rolled snow into balls. "I'd have one on our porch and one coming up behind us, if they can get through the drifts behind the house."

"Same."

"You take the back, I'll take the front." Out of the corner of his eye, he saw Caleb open his mouth and Kentucky glared at him. "Do not make that into something dirty, or I swear I'm going to stuff one of these," he waved the snowball at him, "down your throat, and another down your neck for good measure."

Caleb drew his fingers across his mouth as if he was zipping his lips. "I wasn't going to say a damn thing on the matter."

Sure.

The bombardment of snowballs increased from the front and he knew it was time to move. "On my count."

"Roger."

"Three. Two. One. Go. Go. Go." He exploded out from cover and dived to one side to avoid a direct hit from his lioness, scrambling for purchase on his hands and knees in the snow. "Damn, she's kicking ass up there."

"Why thank you kindly, good sir."

He looked up. "Shit!" He should have known she wouldn't miss the opportunity to have him at her mercy.

Becky smushed a snowball directly onto his face, all the while giggling like a loon.

"You better run, doll face, because I'm coming to get you," he warned softly. At the edge of his mind, he was aware that while she was having an awesome time, it would be way too easy to trigger her into a flashback. He didn't want this awesome day to end like that for her. "I'm coming."

"From what I can see, you are wallowing in the snow." She tossed another snowball in his direction. "Kinda like a pig does in mud. It's cute."

"Cute?" Oh, hell no. There would never be a time when he would ever classify himself as cute. If the other two heard that, they wouldn't ever stop mentioning it. "Don't say that out loud."

"They can't hear us over the sounds of their squabbling."

This time it was him who nailed her with a snowball in a direct hit on the shoulder. She squealed and jumped back, giving him an opening to get to his feet. He stalked up the steps of the porch, using the snowballs to give himself a couple of more seconds to pounce. He staggered back a step when she did the exact opposite to what he had expected and leaped for him, much like she had when he'd arrived at her house in San Diego. Except this time, it wasn't tears of fear she was crying into his neck, but tears of laughter. "Having fun?"

"God, yes."

He banded his arm under her butt as she wrapped her legs around his waist. "I'm going to press you against the door." Sure, telling her took away the element of surprise, but he also enjoyed that moan she made in his ear way too much to care. His mouth hovered over hers and they grinned at each other. "Best Christmas ever."

"Yes. Yes, it is." She tilted her head to one side, her fingers teased at the hair on the back of his neck. "So now you've caught me… what are you going to do with me?"

"This." He captured her lips with his, licking and tasting her mouth until he forgot about everything but her. At least until a snowball landed square on the center of his back.

"I don't think they are snowball fighting anymore," Draven said behind them.

"Me either," Caleb agreed. "Let's go. Leave them to... it." At least one of them had an ounce of common sense.

"Yeah, I don't want to see Mom and Dad smooching and going at it on the porch," Draven replied. "Because, eww, that's my adopted sister."

Huh. What the hell is he talking about?

But he could figure that out later. Kentucky shifted her to get a hand free while making sure she didn't fall and gave them the middle finger.

Nosey fucking bastards. Thank fuck, she's laughing about it.

"Want to go inside?"

"Yes."

He almost *did* drop her when she followed up her single word answer by nipping at his earlobe.

How the hell am I supposed to survive this and do what she needs and not what I want?

He turned his head to capture her lips again. There would never be a time when he had enough of her. She licked at the corner of his mouth, almost bringing him to his knees as he nudged at the door handle with the back of his hand and managed to get it open. "Slow down, doll face," he whispered against her mouth. "We don't have to rush. We have all day..." She cut him off by kissing him deeply as he got them both inside the cabin. Closing the door was a different story, and they both yelped then snorted in laughter into each other's mouths as his hand missed it... twice... before he got it shut, all the while still kissing each other.

"Get these off," Becky growled at him, pulling at the zipper on his coat. She struggled to get down, and he placed her on her feet. How he did that while still kissing her wasn't something either of them noticed.

"Yes." His fingers helped her pull off both their coats.

Their hands seemed to find each other, stroking and petting as they stripped each other, until he was down to his boxers and Becky to her bra and panties. He picked her back up and moved them to the couch. If his butt was sitting down, then she had control… if it was what she needed, then he was man enough to give it to her.

He ran his hands up her back, clasping her to his chest, and smiled at her. "Hey."

"Hey, you."

"You good, baby?"

"Yes." She nodded her head, then kissed the spot she had claimed had a dimple last night. "Thank you for asking."

"Hey, we…" He dipped his chin and kissed the side of her mouth. "We are a team. We move forward when both of us are ready. It's not my timeline or yours… it's ours." He wasn't in a rush; he knew making love to her would happen. With how they set each other on fire, that was their destiny. But he was playing for keeps and would wait for as long as she needed without a second thought. Because he knew it would be epic between them when it did.

Long minutes were spent exploring, finding out which spot was ticklish, and which made the other sigh. He didn't dare move his hips as his dick already ached so freaking bad, if it rubbed on the fabric of his boxers… well then, she might be in for a surprise introduction to his cock insisting she knew it was primed and ready to go. When he could no longer bear it, he kissed her softly and forced himself to pull back. "You shower and I'll go next." There was no way in hell he could get in that shower with her. None. He could take care of himself while she was showering.

"But…"

God, he felt her disappointment right down to his toes. He swept her hair, which had fallen out of her braid, back from her face. "No, doll face, we are not rushing this."

"Sometimes, I really just want to beat you."

"When it's time," he reminded her, "we'll both be ready, and nothing will make us stop. Until then..." He cupped her face with both hands and drew her mouth back to his to plant a hot, deep kiss on her lips. "We figure out what we like. We play, we learn, and we..." He kissed her again. It didn't matter what it did to him. The urgency and need ripped at his soul, but he refused to allow those emotions to win. "Until then, we wait until we are both ready." She smacked at his shoulders, and dear god was her pout sexy as fuck. He almost gave in. Almost, but his need to have her want him as much as he wanted her won out. Oh, there was no doubt she wanted him... but he needed to know she wanted him for him, and not just to see if she was ready for that step. What was between them would not be an experiment, damn it. He would not allow it to be.

"You are the most frustrating man on the planet."

"I know, doll face." He winced when her knee brushed over his dick as she climbed out of his lap to stand next to the couch.

"Someday, I am going to make you follow through." That she wasn't doing it now though, told him he made the right decision. He watched her fabulous ass as she stormed off to the bathroom.

Yup, totally made the right decision.

Once the bathroom door slammed behind her, he pressed one hand against his dick, but even that wasn't enough to ease the ache. He'd take this upstairs just in case she came out of the shower and caught him beating one out.

That could be hot.

Yes, it would be scorching hot. He could admit that to himself, but now was not when he wanted that to happen. He wanted them in his house, in the bed he hoped would be theirs.

When he heard the shower switch on, he got to his feet. He was on the second to last step at the top of stairs when his phone buzzed. "Damn." Maybe it was someone texting to wish him happy holidays, but he couldn't think who else there would be who would do that. He'd spoken to everyone he normally spoke to at Christmas earlier this morning. He didn't really need to go look at the message, but the angry wasps which took flight in his belly told him what he needed to know. When he picked it up, he didn't even have to flip through the screens, as the notification still flashed on the home screen.

Trev: W.U. 4 Hrs. PU. 1 Hr.

He immediately hit forward on the text and sent it to all the members of his team, except for Rexar. The dude was having his first Christmas with his wife and son, there wasn't a hope in hell he was dragging him to some shithole country. "Fuck." Didn't freaking terrorists and assholes ever take a fucking day off?

Apparently not. That was why they were called terrorists and assholes.

He brought the phone upstairs with him and called Trev back. Before he added anyone else to the roster, he needed to clear it with HQ. "Hey, Trev."

"Yo, you are wheels up for A-Stan." In his typical style, Trev didn't wait for him to ask questions. He just went straight to delivering the need-to-know information. "All intel packs will be onboard when you reach Coronado."

"Bro, we're snowed in here. I told you that earlier this morning."

"Yeah, I remember. I have a bird dropping over your location in an hour to take you to base. From there, you are jumping a C-130 onto your target location."

"The boss?"

"He's downstairs in the medical ward with Lina. His ass isn't going anywhere."

"That's one hell of a Christmas present to give a man, isn't it?"

"Yeah," Trev agreed. "If she doesn't murder him first. I can hear the yelling from all the way down here." He snorted out a laugh. "Apparently, the boss isn't getting laid again… ever."

"Ouch." He did not want to be in Nemesis's position today. With a former assassin for a wife and you'd pissed her off, that would be a hell of a dangerous place to be. "I only have limited—"

"All gear will meet you at base, and if there's anything missing, you can grab them from our secondary location."

In other words, if he didn't have enough weapons, then he could hop on over to the base in Pakistan and grab them. Gone were the times they used to have that secondary location in Kabul. But Pakistan worked almost just as well. "Roger that." He remembered why he'd called in the first place. "I need someone to replace Bravo Two on this trip. His situation is similar to the boss's and I'm not…"

"Already covered," Trev interrupted. "The boss cleared for Charlie team volunteers to go with you. Braddock and Lucian will be on the bird that picks you up."

"Awesome." Both Braddock Keane and Lucian Wolf were solid operators. "And my Becky?"

"I can organize for her to stay at that location long term," Trev said. "I'll get with Tex and see if there's any reason that can't happen. Or you can take her with you to San Diego and have Mozart or Wolf pick her up…"

"No." Everything in him rejected the idea of her going back to the house where the asshole had placed shackles on her countertop. "What about Montana?"

"I'm not going to Montana."

He whirled around at the sound of her voice behind him.

"Quit deciding shit for me without talking to me first." She plopped her hands on her hips and glared at him. "If you tell me the options, I can at least make an informed decision without you saying jump and expecting me to ask you how high."

"I'll let you fix that." Trev ended the call. So much for having a brother's back.

"You're leaving?"

It wasn't phrased as the accusation he'd expected, but more of a question. He sat on the end of the bed and patted the spot next to him. "Come sit with me."

"Where are you going?" She did as he asked, and when he lifted his arm, she snuggled into his side.

"I can't tell you that." He rubbed his chin on top of her damp hair. "This is the job, doll face. Someone calls and I leave. I can't tell you where I'm going, when I'll be back. I can't even tell you when or if I'll be able to call you."

"Well, that more than sucks."

"Yes, it does." He'd never realized it before. Having someone like Becky waiting for him to come home was a whole different ball game to having his mom waiting to know if he was back or not. "Please be patient with me." He squeezed his arm around her a little tighter. "This having someone to come home to is new to me, too."

She glanced up at him with confusion written all over her face. "Umm, I thought you'd been doing, you know, for years."

He chuckled softly. "Yeah. I have. For more years than I haven't. I mean the having someone other than Ma waiting for me."

"No previous wife, or long-term girlfriend?"

He shook his head. "I didn't want to leave anyone behind when stuff was shit over there and we never knew if we were coming back or not."

"But you'd leave me behind?"

Yeah, he'd known as soon as the words were out of his mouth that would be her next question. "You are different." How did he make her understand? "Having you waiting here means I'll fight harder and longer to be able to come home to you." He hoped he wasn't making a total mess of this. "Not that I'm saying anyone in my past wasn't worth similar. They were for someone else… not me."

"My hero," she quipped, as if she was trying not to let her true feelings show.

He understood the need to deflect. He just didn't want that from her. He wanted and needed more. He tipped up her chin. "I don't think you do get it. You are not a princess who needs me to come riding in on some fancy white steed to save you. You, my heart, are a warrior who needs a safe place to rest between the battles which rage around you." Kentucky pressed a kiss to the center of her forehead. "I want to you see me as that safe place. I am your home, not your damn hero. Got it?"

"Yes, I have it." She placed her hand over his heart. The look in her eyes as she met his slayed him. "You are my home, and I am yours?"

"Exactly." From where they sat on the end of the bed, he could just about make out the hands on the clock. The second hand mocked him as it counted down the minutes he had left.

Tick tock. Tick tock.

"I need to know what you want to do," he told her. "Do you want to come with us to San Diego, or maybe go stay with Caroline and the others in Riverton, or stay here?" He loved she didn't just give him a fast answer, and she really thought about the question. While he waited, that damn clock kept right on mocking him.

Tick fucking tock.

"I don't know which is safest," she finally said, "do you?"

"Me either," he admitted. "Let me call Tex and see if he knows. Trev already said he doesn't when I was talking to him."

"Okay, call him."

He picked up the phone he'd discarded on the bed and punched in the number—okay, he pressed one number as speed-dial—and waited for the call to connect. "Hey, Tex."

"Hey, man, everything okay?"

"Yeah, first, Happy Christmas. Am I interrupting you?"

"Many happy returns, and no, I was just talking to a friend online as she kicks my ass in this game we are playing."

"Someone is kicking your butt at computer shit?" He hadn't known that was even possible. "Tell me who she is so I can tell Nemesis to hire her."

"Hell no," Tex growled in a possessive manner which made Kentucky's eyebrows shoot almost into his hairline.

"Whoa, I'm kidding. We aren't going to steal your friend out from under your nose."

"Good, because I'd hate to have to kill you," Tex replied. "Finding gators to dispose of bodies sucks right now."

"I'll bet."

"What do you need me for?"

"I have to go to work." He knew Tex would understand what that meant. "Me and Becky are trying to figure out where is the safest place for her."

"Montana."

Jeez, he didn't even think about that one. But then, neither did I.

He glanced at Becky. Not that he thought she'd have changed her mind, but she needed to be included in the decision-making process and had to suppress a growl when she shook her head. "And if Montana is off the table?"

"Then I'm going to take off my leg and beat Nemesis over the head with it," Tex deadpanned.

"I'd hold him for you if that was the reason it's off the table."

"The women we love are going to be the death of me."

In the background, Kentucky could hear the tapping of a keyboard. "How safe is here? Because I think we both agree that San Diego is definitely not as safe as either of us would like."

"I totally agree." Tex's keyboard kept on filtering through the phone. "I'm trying to see if there are cameras there, and if she's agreeable, I can keep an eye on her?"

"There's two on the main office." Kentucky gave him a rundown of what he saw when they first arrived. "Caleb should have a couple of sets in his ruck. He normally has some game cameras at least."

"If he has those, then I can keep an eye on the place," Tex offered. "But only if your lady agrees. I won't invade her privacy or make her feel bad for anything."

Kentucky glanced at her, and she nodded in agreement. "Okay. I'll leave her a phone with your number programed into it." As he spoke, he reached into his go-bag for the spare phone Rexar had given him. He powered it on and opened the text box. "What's your number, bro?" He tapped it into the phone and shot off a text to Tex. "That's the number."

"Got it."

"I'll get with Trev and see how I can get access to those cameras. Between us, we'll keep her as safe as possible."

"I appreciate it—"

"Stop," Tex cut him off. "When you find that special someone, we all get to help keep them safe. They are the reason we fight to come home."

To hear Tex echoing what he'd told Becky a few minutes

ago hopefully reinforced it for her. "Still, I owe you. If you call, I'll come on the run."

"I'll add you to my ever-growing list." Tex snorted. "I got your lady. Go do your thing, bro, and we'll catch up when you get back."

"Thanks, man."

"No worries." Tex ended the call.

Kentucky tapped out a text to Caleb, asking him to put up the cameras he had in the blind spots surrounding the cabin, and then a second one to Trev, reminding him to fix and pay for the cabin, at least until he got back. Both men immediately confirmed they would do as he asked, and Kentucky shut off his phone.

"I can stay here?"

"Yes, for now at least." He hugged her close. "We're booked until the end of January. If it needs to be longer, Trev will extend the dates if possible."

"Okay."

"If he can't, promise me you'll go to Montana."

"You don't think you will be back before the end of the month?"

Damn, he should have known she'd be fast on the uptake. "I don't know. I'm just preparing as if I'm not going to be, so you aren't jumping around from place to place."

"Thank you." She squeezed her arms around him. "I don't know what else to say, but thank you for all you do for me."

"It's my pleasure, doll face." He glanced at the clock. Crap, time really was running faster today. "I'm gonna put snow chains on the truck outside for you." He reluctantly got to his feet. "Don't try to pull the other one out of the ditch until either the snow melts or the owners come back. Promise me."

"I promise."

It would have to be enough. Especially as he knew she didn't want to be locked away anywhere again. He couldn't blame her for it. If he'd been locked in a container for months on end, the last thing he would want to be was behind gates or bars again. Even if those gates were Texas gates on the road to Nemesis Ranch. "I gotta finish getting ready..."

"Go." She kissed him, a swift peck on the lips. "I'll pack you up some cookies and make some sandwiches with the leftover ham." Her smile was a little forced, but he understood why. "Butter, not mayo for you, right?"

"Yes, please." He watched her go down the stairs and glared at the damn clock. He needed to hustle if he wanted the chains on the truck before he had to leave.

He'd just closed the locks on the last set of chains when he heard the *whoop - whoop* of an approaching helo. "Caleb. Bird is incoming."

"Here." Caleb appeared around the side of the cabin where Kentucky and he had taken cover during the snowball fight a few hours ago. "All set, and I've texted Trev the Wi-Fi codes. As long as they keep getting signal, both he and Tex can access them."

"Thank you." He'd never been more grateful to have the men he did as friends and brothers. "I appreciate it."

"Fuck off, Ken." Draven dropped his and Caleb's go-bags near the wheel of the truck. "She's yours, so she's family and we protect our own."

He knew that. Hell, he preached it to almost every attached man in Nemesis and the SEALs down in Riverton. But this time, when he was the one on the receiving end, it meant that much more. He opened his arms for Becky as she came racing out of the cabin. "Come here, you."

"Before you both go getting teary." Draven tugged her away from him and gave her a fast hug. "I want my turn."

"Here." She handed Draven a paper bag. "I made you something in case you get hungry on the way."

"Aww, she likes me."

"Idiot." Becky hugged him once more before pulling away and handing a bag to Caleb. She hugged him, too. "Be safe. Both of you."

Kentucky was relieved that she was back in his arms in time for him to breathe her in before he had to leave. He already knew he'd be going up the rope, as the clearing here wasn't big enough for the bird to land.

"Promise me you will be safe," she whispered against the side of his neck.

"I will if you will."

"I will."

Kentucky kissed her soundly. He wanted her to remember it. Remember him. Just as he knew, he'd need this kiss to get him through some long nights in the days to come. He took the bag she offered him and closed his eyes tight against the rotor wash he could now feel against the top of his head. His time was up. "I gotta go." He raised his voice to be heard over the noise of the helicopter.

"I know. Be safe and I'll see you when I see you."

He reluctantly let her go and turned to follow Draven and Caleb up the rope. The man on the door went to shut it behind him as soon as his butt cleared the entrance, but he put his hand up, silently asking him to wait.

The doorman gave him a thumbs up, telling him he understood as the helo rose high enough to clear the tree line.

"Thanks." Kentucky leaned out. He felt someone grab onto his belt and appreciated the assistance. Falling from here might not kill him, but it would absolutely suck for sure. He scanned the yard right up to the porch of their cabin, and his heart jumped when he saw Becky waving at him. He waved back, but within seconds she had disappeared from view and he pulled his head back inside. "Appreciate it, bro."

"New spouse?" The dude slammed the door shut and secured the latch.

"Yeah, something like that."

CHAPTER TWENTY-THREE

Becky smiled at her student through the video. "Remember, Jodie. When you speak in English, we don't always pronounce all the letters." She'd reminded her of the same thing every day for the last two weeks since Tex and Trev had helped her set up teaching classes online. It made her feel a lot more secure that they vetted each student. Was it legal? She wasn't entirely sure. But if they hadn't been able to confirm who the student was, she wasn't sure she'd have been able to take this first step back into her real life. She glanced at the clock on the bottom of the screen. "That's enough for today," she informed Jodie. "We've gone over by a few minutes as it is, and I need to run to the grocery store."

"I'm sorr—"

"No, no. Don't worry at all." She waved her off. Jodie was a high school student in Germany who hoped to go to do an exchange year into a school in the United States, but needed her English to be better. "I'm happy to help. I just have to run to the store before it closes, as I'm out of tea."

"Thank you, Ms. Becky."

"You're welcome. I'll see you at the same time next week."

She ended the Zoom call and got to her feet. After a quick stop at the bathroom, she grabbed her keys and her purse. It had taken almost two full weeks for the snow to melt enough for her to get the other truck out of the snowbank and parked outside her cabin. And now that they were almost to the middle of February and there was still a little snow on the ground, she kept using the truck with the chains on the tires. She didn't care if the locals were zooming past her. Driving on snow was not her favorite thing in the world to do. But her options were to sit here and starve, ask the owners to do her grocery shopping, or drive the truck. She chose to drive the truck, because who wanted someone else picking out the tomato which suited them best?

"Hi, Becky." The owner paused in sweeping the snow off her porch. "Is everything okay over with you?"

"Hey, Mrs. Zorastrian. Yes, it is. Do you need anything at the store? I have to run out for a bit."

"Not at all. You be careful on that bend before the bridge. My Jack said there was some black ice there when he went out for the paper earlier."

Crap.

"I will, thank you." She hit the button on the keys to open the truck and climbed in. She didn't bother tying her seat belt yet—she needed to half stand out of the seat so she could see enough to reverse out of the spot. Not that there were any other vehicles to hit, as she was the only guest. But still, she didn't want to get in the habit, as the last thing she needed was for Tuck to come back and find a big dent in his rental truck.

Finally, she was out of the spot, sat into the seat, and strapped on her seat belt. She waved at Mrs. Zorastrian and headed for town.

Please don't be bad.

Please don't be bad.

"It's freaking ice. Just drive slowly and you will be fine." She knew it was there, so she was prepared. She'd probably never driven as slowly as she did on that road trip to town, but she didn't even care. Getting to her destination safely was more important than getting there fast. The a-hole in the dirty pickup truck could just go shove his head down a toilet or something. He was being mean and grumpy by blowing his horn nonstop in an attempt to get her to speed up. "If you hit me from behind, you are the one in the wrong, buddy. I bet you wouldn't do that if it was a man behind the wheel instead of me."

Finally, they reached the single traffic light in town and the pickup pulled into the other lane next to her. Becky glimpsed the man out of the corner of her eye as he glared at her. "Ugh, could you be any more creepy, jerk?" Thankfully, he was taking the left, and she was going straight ahead to the store. She turned on the flicker and pulled into the store's parking lot. Finding a space she could drive into was easier than she thought, and she breathed out a sigh of relief. She refused to worry about the journey home until she had to.

It didn't take her long to run around the store and grab the few items she needed. Of course, this was one of the times she'd convinced herself that she didn't need a basket, and as she hurried to the self-service checkout, she had to juggle to ensure she didn't drop anything.

Next time, bring a freaking basket.

"Please don't do this to me."

She dropped all of her items on the shelf next to the checkout and glanced over her shoulder at the woman behind her. Over the woman's shoulder, she could see the red box. She knew exactly what that red box meant. "Are you okay?" She stepped over to the woman. "Is it being finicky with your card?" She hated that this woman was attempting to buy a pot noodle and two apples and her card was declined.

"I'm sorry, Ma'am." One of the clerks she'd seen a few times before came over to the checkouts. "Unless you have another way to pay, I'm going to have to ask you to leave the items here."

"I—" The woman swallowed hard and turned to leave the store. "I'm so sorry." She put her card back into her wallet.

"Excuse me." There was no way Becky was letting this happen. When she'd been having the worst time of her life, complete strangers had stepped up to help her. They were still helping her, even though she'd only heard from Kentucky once in all these weeks. "Let me put your items through with mine..."

"No. No. I can't ask you to do that." The woman managed a small smile. "But I appreciate the offer." Without giving her time to plead with her, she turned again and walked out the doors.

"Can I have those, Mike?" She pointed to the items the woman had tried to pay for. "I'm going to put them through with my groceries and see if I can catch her."

"That's very nice of you, Ma'am."

She took the items and scanned them through, then scanned her own stuff before feeding cash into the machine. Why did the receipt take forever to print when she was in a hurry? She tossed everything into a carrier bag and hurried outside. "Where did you go?" She turned to the left and then the right, trying to catch a glimpse of the woman. "Oh, no." She should have been quicker to get through the checkout and out of the store. Becky made her way back to the truck. She wanted to help, dang it.

She pressed the brakes and slowed to a stop at the exit of the parking lot and glanced left and right. As she did, a woman carrying a suitcase walking in the opposite direction to where she needed to go caught her eye. "There you are." She changed the direction of her flicker and took off after her. "This poor woman is going to think you've lost your mind." But at this point, she didn't even care. She just knew that she had to help if she was able. She hit the button on the window as she drew level with the woman. "Excuse me. Excuse me, Ma'am."

The woman paused and looked at her, confusion all over her face when she clearly recognized her. "I—"

"I have your items," Becky cut her off. "Please take them. I only want to help, because I know what it's like to have nothing and nobody to care if I disappear or not. Please."

Isn't that the understatement of the year?

"Why do you care?" the woman asked. "Nobody ever cares."

What she wouldn't do to be able to take that bleak tone out of her voice. If anyone needed a friend, it was this woman. Becky couldn't care less that she was overstepping. Well, she did... but she didn't let it stop her. The poor thing was shivering in that thin coat. "Let me buy you a coffee." She pointed to the red building down the street, a couple of buildings from where they were. "At least sit and have a warm drink, even if it's only for a few minutes. I want nothing from you, just a few minutes of your time. I want to make sure you are okay."

"Why do you care?" the woman repeated.

"I don't know." She wasn't above admitting she had no clue what she was doing. Which probably wasn't her smartest move, considering her background. "I just know that I do."

"What's in it for you?" She didn't blame her for being wary. Just because Becky was a woman didn't mean she didn't have the potential to be dangerous.

"Nothing but someone to talk to for a few minutes.

Someone who doesn't live inside a computer screen, that is. My boyfriend—" Could she call Kentucky a boy? Or even her boyfriend? She didn't know how else to describe him, so she decided in this instance it was perfectly okay to take a little poetic license. "—Is away with his work, and won't be back for a few weeks. It gets kind of lonely around here when I'm considered a blow-in and I don't know anyone."

"I'm guessing a blow-in means you weren't born and raised here and only arrived not so long ago."

"Yes, that's exactly what it is." Becky nodded. "We moved here the day before Christmas and Ken got called away on Christmas night." She didn't want to use the name she called Kentucky with a complete stranger. She had that much common sense, at least. "Why don't we go in and have that coffee?" Was she being pushy? Yes, yes, she was. But she was doing her best to help, so the little voice inside her which said she was overstepping way too much could just back off.

Thankfully, the woman finally relented. "Okay. I suppose one coffee won't hurt."

"Thank you." She drove along beside the woman at walking pace, afraid if she went on ahead that the other woman would disappear again, and parked directly in front of the door of the café. After a quick rummage through the grocery bag, she came up with the items the woman had tried to pay for, along with some cereal bars and cookies she'd bought as a treat for herself, and stuffed them into one of the many totes she kept in the pocket on the door. Not that she ever remembered to bring them into a store with her, but they were there in case she did actually remember she not only owned them, but to use them. When she got out of the truck, she was relieved to see the other woman waiting for her next to the door with her suitcase at her feet. "Thank you so much for waiting. I'm Becky." She held out the tote.

"No, no. I couldn't possibly..."

"Please take them." Becky opened the door of the café and waited for her to go ahead. "If you don't, I will eat that whole package of cookies, and my hips really don't need to have a sniff of them, never mind the results of what would happen if I ate them all."

The woman sighed, as if she finally realized that Becky would not take no for an answer. "Well, thank you. I appreciate it more than you know."

"You're welcome…" she trailed off, hoping the other woman would tell her her name.

"Summer." She slapped her hand off her forehead. "God, I'm an idiot. My name is Summer Pack."

"Nice to meet you, Summer." Becky smiled at her. "Like I said, I'm Becky. Becky Jones." The boys were going to be so fricking mad with her for giving away so much information to a complete stranger. She just knew it. "May I have a large latte please, and a grilled cheese? Summer, what would you like?"

"Just a latte, please."

"Make that two lattes and two sandwiches, please." She ignored Summer's protests and glanced around the almost empty café. "We'll be over there at the table with the red tablecloth by the wall."

"Of course." The lady behind the counter smiled at them. "I'll bring your coffees over to you right away, but your sandwiches will be about ten minutes. Is that okay?"

"Perfect." She led Summer to the table she'd pointed out to the girl behind the counter. "Come, come. Sit, sit."

"You're very bossy." Summer took the seat across from her. "You know that, right?"

"Why, yes, yes I do." When the corners of Summer's lips quirked upward, she smiled back at her. "But I've been here by myself since Christmastime and it's nice to talk to someone who isn't either on the phone or on the other side of a computer screen."

"Why me?"

"Because you look like you're lovely and you aren't going to kidnap me."

Summer snorted in laughter. She leaned back when the server brought their coffee, giving her room to put it on the table. "Kidnapping isn't part of my resume. Now if you want to know the ins and outs of a Fortune 500, I used to be your girl... Not anymore, though."

"Ah." That made sense. She was totally reading between the lines and making assumptions here, but she thought maybe Summer had lost her job recently. "I'm sorry."

"Don't be." Summer sipped her coffee and shuddered as if the heat from it was welcome as it hit her tummy. "Divorce, no more corporate, and being an idiot, I decided I might as well hit the road and see where it takes me."

"All roads lead to Big Bear?"

"When my car broke down, I saw a poster for Big Bear Lake cabins. They had a help wanted sign, so I grabbed a bus here. But I was hungry and decided to grab some food from the store..." She hid her face behind her coffee mug. "You saw what happened there."

"I think there comes a time in every girl's life when she wants to run away from home. Just pack your crap, throw it in the car, and go until the car drives no more. I know I have more than once."

"Pipe dreams don't always turn out so well." Summer frowned at the sandwich the server placed in front of her, but said nothing until Becky had thanked the girl and they were alone again. Summer pushed the plate across the table toward Becky. "Here you go."

"Oh, that one is for you." Becky picked up her sandwich and took a bite. "I couldn't possibly eat both of them. If you aren't hungry, we can get a go-bag and you can take it with you later."

"Why do I feel like you are… I don't know what you are." Summer sipped more of her coffee.

"Right." Becky grinned at her. "I'm right. And we both know that grilled cheese never tastes as good when it's reheated, so you might as well eat it now."

"Okay, okay. You twisted my arm," Summer agreed finally. "Someday, I hope someone sees you when you need help and they do it."

"They already have," Becky admitted. "When I was in a place where I needed someone so bad, a complete stranger gave it to me."

"I'm glad." Summer sighed happily after the first bite of her food. "Do you still talk to them?"

"To him." Becky didn't need the mirror across from them to know she was blushing and smiling at the same time. "Yes, I do. But he's working, so it will be a while before I do again."

Summer looked at her with curiosity on her face, before understanding dawned. "The boyfriend."

"Yes—"

"Excuse me, ladies." The girl from the counter carried over a receipt. "I'm sorry, but we're closing in a few minutes. Do you mind settling your bill so I can cash up?"

"Of course not." Becky glanced at the bill and reached for her purse. "Summer, do you have somewhere to stay tonight?"

"Um…"

She just knew that the answer was no. Inspiration struck as she pulled money out to pay. "Miss, do you know the Zorastrians? They have the cabins down below the bridge?"

"I do, why?"

"I'm staying there with them," Becky said. "Would you mind taking my new friend Summer's details, and if she doesn't come back in here tomorrow to confirm she's okay, will you call the police and say she's missing?"

"I'll call Mrs. Zee and confirm," the girl said. "I'm not agreeing to anything until I know you are actually staying there." She took the cash from Becky. "I'll bring you back your change in a jiffy."

"What are you doing?" Summer hissed.

"It's way too cold still for you to camp out," Becky reminded her. "Spring hasn't even hit here properly yet. If you have no place to go, you'll catch your death from the cold."

"You…"

"No," Becky cut her off. "You are coming to stay with me for the night and we'll figure out where to find your Big Bear Lake cabins in the morning." She was totally out of line, and she absolutely knew it. But Summer needed help, and she was lonely. It would be nice to have someone in the cabin with her, even if it was only for one night. "Please let me help you, just this once."

"I'm counting that, and we are up to at least three times today already." Summer glared at her. "Are you one of these friends who just waltzes in and fixes everything, even if it doesn't need fixing?"

"Ummm…."

"You totally are." Summer sighed. "I'm not going to win this round, am I?"

Becky slowly shook her head. "I'd never be able to sleep if I knew you were outside sleeping God knows where. Not knowing if you were cold or sick or…"

"Okay, okay." Summer gave in. "If the server says you're legit, I'll take you up on your kind offer." She pointed the sandwich she held in her hand at Becky. "If you turn into a serial killer, I'm going to be so pissed and I'll haunt you forever."

"I promise, I'm not." Becky was relieved that Summer would come home with her. She'd cheerfully pay Mrs. Z. some extra if it was needed.

"Mrs. Zorastrian says bring her on home with you." The server placed the change on the table next to Becky's plate and then handed a paper bag to them. "She asked that you bring these for her, too."

"Thank you." Becky smiled at her. "I appreciate your help." She pushed the change back to the edge of the table. "That's for you."

"Thank you, Ma'am." The server turned to Summer. "May I take your details, so I have them on file if you don't show up tomorrow?"

Summer nodded and pulled out her driver's license. The server quickly jotted the details down in her notebook. "We close at seven tomorrow. If you aren't in here by then, I'll go to the station with this." She glanced at Becky. "Mrs. Z. has your details, so I'll get them from her if I need to."

They watched her walk away and went back to finishing their coffee and sandwiches, chitchatting and making small talk until it was time to leave.

* * *

"This is us." Becky turned the nose of the truck in the driveway to the cabins. "They aren't fancy," she warned, suddenly nervous. "But they are cozy."

"I'd be grateful even if it was a toolshed connected to the cabin." Summer shivered despite the heat which blew full blast in the cab of the truck. "I'm not picky."

"Me either." She parked in her usual spot and by the time she'd switched off the engine, Mrs. Z. was standing on the front porch of the office building. "Hi." Becky grabbed the bag from the café and her groceries. "Mrs. Z., this is Summer Pack. Summer, Mrs. Zorastrian, the owner."

"Nice to meet you, Summer." Mrs. Zorastrian took the paper bag from Becky. "It's lovely for our Becky to have a friend over to stay. You know where to find me if you need anything. Do you have enough blankets, Becky?"

"I do, Mrs. Z., thank you." Becky waved and led the way to her tiny home. She could be making a big mistake by bringing a complete stranger home with her. But in her defense, after all the help she'd received, she hadn't been able to help herself. She didn't see a stranger. She saw a woman needing a helping hand, and she needed to be able to do something to fix it.

"I appreciate all you're doing for me." Summer placed her suitcase next to the door. "More than you know."

"I know, don't worry about it at all." Becky showed her the kitchen and led the way to the bathroom. "Why don't you have a warm shower and put on some clean clothes?" she offered. "I know it's not much, but it's cold and you might feel better after it."

"Do you mind?"

"Absolutely not." There should never be a time when a shower and changing into clean clothes was a luxury. "Help yourself to whatever you need from under the sink in the bathroom."

"Thank you."

Becky started putting away the groceries she had purchased, and as soon as she heard the shower switch on, she made herself some tea and picked up the phone. She might really want to help Summer, but she wasn't entirely stupid. As Kentucky was out of reach, she needed to call Tex and see if there was anything she needed to worry about. She sat in one chair and placed her mug on the arm, then dialed the number and waited for it to connect.

"Hi, Tex, it's Becky."

"What's wrong?"

She should have expected that to be his first reaction. Normally, he called her to check in and make sure she was okay, and not the other way around. "No. No. Nothing is wrong, but..." She quickly explained the situation to him. "I just wanted you to know..."

"Give me a minute. I'm gonna have a sneaky look at her background."

Tex's wariness made her second-guess every decision she'd made. "Thank you."

"I'm telling you now, though. Smith is gonna be pissed as all get out that you brought a stranger home with you. Even if that stranger is a woman."

"She's lost, Tex," Becky chided him softly. "She reminds me of me when I first moved down to San Diego."

"I know, and I get it." She could hear his fingers flying over the keyboards. "I can't find anything which screams red flag at me."

Oh, thank God, I didn't screw up.

"That's a good thing, right?"

"Yeah, but it doesn't mean it was the smart thing to do," Tex reminded her. "Ken..."

"I'll handle Kentucky," Becky pushed back. "I'm not trying to do a stupid, I'm trying to help someone who looks like they are in trouble just like I've had been in the past."

Tex's inhale was loud enough that it was harsh and audible in her ear. "Do you think Summer was trafficked?"

"No." From what Summer had told her, she didn't think she had been. But hearing Tex put it like that hit her hard, and she rubbed at the ache in her chest. "She's just down on her luck and I can help, like Kentucky, and everyone helped me."

"I can see why you want to do that," Tex agreed. "It should be okay. I can't find anything that makes my skin crawl."

"Good." She trusted his instincts more than she did her own at this point. She blew across the top of the mug and took a sip of her tea. One benefit of drinking it outside was it cooled down faster so she could drink it.

"I can pay for a cabin for her until she can go to the other campground to ask about the job you mentioned."

He is the sweetest man on the planet next to my Tuck.

"No, I think it's okay." Becky was mostly refusing his generous offer because she was lonely, but she also liked Summer. She'd like to think her radar for trouble wasn't totally broken. Having Tex offer to pay for accommodation for Summer confirmed it.

"I want you to check in every hour," Tex told her. "If I don't get a text, I'm sending the police around there to check on you."

"Every two hours," she bargained. "And I tell you when I go to sleep and what time I set my alarm for, as I'm not staying up all night..." She paused and added on, "Unless you think it's absolutely necessary?"

"Maybe I'm being over cautious," Tex agreed. "But I promised Kentucky that nothing would happen to you on my watch. Please make it easier on me by sticking to your offer."

"You agree?" She wasn't sure if that was what he meant. "Every two hours and I tell you when I go to sleep and what time I set my alarm clock for?" She wanted to be very sure she didn't screw up and make him freak out or worry unnecessarily.

"Yes," Tex confirmed.

Maybe they were both being overly cautious, but she was grateful he took her seriously when she said Summer just needed a friend to be there for her. Most men wouldn't have been, at least in her past experience. "I can do that."

"Deal." Tex's voice was filled with approval. "I'll text you and you respond with a different emoji every time. So I know it's you."

"Perfect. Thank you, Tex."

"Call me if you get any weird feelings..."

"I promise if the voodoo gods come calling or whispering in my ear, yours will be the first number I call."

"Keep that snark, Becks." Tex snorted a laugh. "It suits you."

"On that note...."

"Oh, one more thing. Thank you for the box of cookies Fee and Alabama sent me. They were awesome. You had a good plan that time."

"Yay. You're welcome. Bye, Tex."

"Later."

She picked up her mug and went back in the house just as Summer was coming out of the bathroom. "Would you like tea, coffee, or wine?" She could at least pretend she still had social skills, even if they were rusty.

"Um." Summer hesitated and drew in a breath so deep Becky saw her shoulders heave. "It's probably the most reckless option, but I'd love some wine."

"Red or white?"

"White, please."

Becky totally understood the nervousness, they were complete strangers, after all. "Make yourself at home. If you want to sit on the sofa, then sit on the sofa. If you'd prefer to sit at the table, then that's good, too." She grabbed a bottle of wine from the fridge and poured a glass each for them. "I have a sausage casserole in the crock-pot. I hope that's okay for dinner."

"Thanks." Summer took the glass and held it between

both hands. "You don't have to feed me again. You've done enough as it is already."

"Shh, we're going to watch something ridiculously funny on the TV, drink our wine, and chill. No pressure, no drama."

The next few hours were both awesome and weird. Having someone else in the house answering her comments or questions when she'd spoken to herself out loud made her both jump and then grin. Summer was funny and smart, and she reminded her a lot of the other women she'd met since she'd been rescued with Willow.

After two full seasons of *Friends* reruns and dinner, which had been comfort food at its best, Summer yawned for the third time. Becky slapped her hands on her thighs. "I'm so tired. Do you mind if I go to bed?"

"No. Not at all," Summer replied. "I'm exhausted, too."

Becky went to the small closet under the stairs and grabbed some blankets and a spare pillow. "The couch pulls out into a bed, but I'm not sure how that works."

"I'm so tired, I don't have the energy to figure it out." Summer took the blankets. "I'll just curl up here."

"Okay. Night, Summer."

"Becky?"

"Yes?" She paused on the bottom step and glanced at her houseguest.

"Thank you for helping me."

"You're welcome. Call me if you need me."

"Good night."

Becky had just changed into her jammies when her phone pinged. She'd expected to be annoyed by the check-in, but knowing they were coming had helped her relax and know she had someone in her corner in case something went wrong. This time she picked a smiling wide, emoji and a sleeping one.

Becky: We're going to sleep. I'm setting my alarm for 7.30 AM.

Tex: Awesome. Night, Becks.

Becky. Night, Tex. Tks for everything.

Tex: Welcome.

She placed the phone on the bed right next to her pillow. It didn't happen very often, but if Kentucky called or texted, she didn't want to miss it. Down below in the living room, she could hear Summer setting up her bed on the couch. Becky lay back on the pillow, then turned over onto her side, and opened the phone to the messages screen to read back on previous ones Kentucky had sent her.

CHAPTER TWENTY-FOUR

Tired didn't even begin to describe how exhausted his bones were. The next time the CIA wanted Nemesis to protect a high value asset, Kentucky's team better not be the ones on duty. No, sir, he was officially done with anything which the CIA stuck their noses into. He glanced at the ground as it flew past them; he almost didn't recognize the place. All the snow from Christmas had melted. The flowers were out in full force, and everything was green. The Big Bear area was beautiful in the snow, but now, with the land coming back to life after its freezing winter, it was stunning.

"Bravo One, we're coming up on your target zone in about sixty seconds," Dee warned from the cockpit. "Get ready to bail as soon as we're overhead. Because I already know we can't land this puppy in the clearing that you've got."

Only Dee-Dee would call this helo a puppy. But pilots were freaking weird, so what did he know? "Yes, Ma'am. I'm ready to fast rope my ass outta here when you give the word."

"On target, Bravo One."

"Thanks for the ride, Dee-Dee."

"You're welcome, Bravo One. Now get your ass off my puppy. I'm ready to go home."

He opened the door, took off his comms unit, and handed it to Tate, who was closest to him. Kentucky hooked onto the rope and slid out, diving the others in the helo a saucy salute. They still had the trip to Montana in front of them... but his ass was officially home. He glanced at the cabin as he slid down the rope, waiting for Becky to appear. Disappointment slammed him in the belly when the door stayed shut and no woman came out to see. It was then he noticed one truck was missing.

You should have called her first, dumbass.

There was no doubt he should have, but he'd wanted to surprise her. He bent his knees to brace the impact of landing on the ground and unclipped the rope which attached him to the helo. After giving the guys a thumbs up, he moved away from underneath the helicopter and the rotor wash it sent his way.

"Oh my, Mr. Smith, you do know how to make an entrance." She fanned her hand in front of her face. "It's a sight for this old momma's heart to see a fine man jumping out of a chopper to come visit his girl."

She better not be flirting with me, or I'm telling Becky and sending her after her with some kind of weapon.

"Hey, Mrs. Zorastrian. How are you doing?" He smiled at the owner and crossed the yard to talk to her for a second. "Do you know where my Becky is?"

That's right... remind her you have Becky.

"She went to take her friend Summer up to Big Bear Lake Cabins," Mrs. Zorastrian said. "Summer has an interview for a job there, and Becky wanted to make sure she made it there okay."

Who the hell is Summer?

"Awesome." He wasn't going to let the owners know he did not know who Becky's friend was. He was pretty damn sure when the guys had booked the cabins that they'd put it under his name. It would be weird for him to know his 'wife's' friends. "I'll see her when she gets back."

"She's coming now, dearie." Mrs. Zorastrian pointed toward the entrance to the property. "You better…"

Kentucky barely jumped out of the way in time to avoid being hit by the fender of the truck when Becky screeched to a stop in front of the office.

"Tuck!" Becky squealed and flew out of the truck, racing toward him with a wide smile and joy all over her face.

Kentucky opened his arms and braced for impact as she slammed into his chest. "Hey, doll face."

"You didn't tell me you were coming." Her arms wrapped around his waist and bunched into the material of his coat, as if making sure he didn't disappear again. "I missed you."

"I missed you, too, baby." He drew back so he could see her beautiful face and cupped her cheek with one hand. "I really fucking missed you."

She stepped up on her tippy toes and kissed him. At first it was soft and tentative, but when she jumped, he caught her and she wrapped her legs around his waist, deepening the kiss.

"Aww. Isn't that the sweetest thing?"

Crap, we are outside.

He ignored the sighs from Mrs. Zorastrian and walked toward the cabin, all the while with Becky pressing kisses across his face.

"Go on, dearies, I'll close the truck and keep the keys over here for you."

Shit. The truck.

It wasn't often he forgot about security crap, but right now he didn't care about any truck, never mind locking one.

Even if it was Becky's. He cared about the woman in his arms. Hopefully, Mrs. Zorastrian would take his silence for agreement.

"If you stop this time," Becky grabbed both sides of his face in her hands, "I swear to God I'm going to murder you in your sleep."

Thank fuck.

"I'm not stopping unless you tell me to," he promised. "Not this time. I need you too much."

Her breath fanned hotly across his face as he got them inside and up the stairs. "I don't want to move too fast–" Kentucky couldn't remember what he'd been about to say and he growled when Becky pressed tightly against him, the vee between her thighs rubbing against his rapidly filling erection.

"You're not," Becky reassured him. "If anything, you are moving too slow."

"Still sassy and still bossy as fuck," he growled. "I fucking love it." He lowered her onto the bed and she squeezed her thighs together as if she was trying to find some relief. But clearly it wasn't enough, as she glanced up at him and beckoned him closer. "Oh, yeah?" she breathed out.

"Yes."

"Too much?"

He never wanted to hear that uncertainty in her voice again. "No." He paused and leaned down to kiss her. When he pulled back, they were both breathless. "Hell no, never too much."

A smile spread across her lips, and her eyes darkened with pleasure. "Please," she begged. "I want you. I *need* you."

"Baby, you have no idea how much I want and need you, too," he told her. He stripped down to his boxers while she watched. Kentucky was sure he wasn't imagining he could feel the heat from her gaze as it devoured every inch he uncovered. "Is there room for me on that bed, too?"

"Yes." She scooted up the bed and over to one side, making room for him to climb in. He encouraged her to turn over on her side and curled around her with his hands wrapped around her, gently caressing her stomach.

"You're going to drag this out, aren't you?" Becky shifted against him. That simple touch made his cock throb and his skin break out into goose bumps.

"Yes." Kentucky pressed a kiss to the side of her neck. He should be embarrassed by how quickly he was leaking, but all he could think about was touching her. Loving her. "You're so soft," he murmured as he pulled her closer. Every inch of her body was soft and hot against his chest. He pushed forward a little, letting his cock slide against her leggings-covered ass.

"Keep holding onto me." Her voice was ragged as she reached behind her, digging her fingers into his side as if she needed him inside her skin. "It feels so good being pressed against you while you do that."

"While I explore your body?" he asked as he did just that. Keeping her grounded in the here and now was priority number one. He wanted this to be amazing for them both. She arched her back when he cupped her breast and ran his thumb over her pebbled nipple. "Answer me, baby. While I explore your body?" Kentucky growled softly and ground his erection against her. He kissed the back of her neck and nipped the sensitive spot he knew was just below her ear. She whimpered when he scraped his teeth along the same spot.

"You sound like you want to devour me like the big bad wolf from the fairy tales."

"I'm no wolf, bad or otherwise," Kentucky muttered. "I'm just your man. Yours."

"I want you to devour me." She twisted to look at him over her shoulder. "I want my memories to be of you. Of us."

Fuck. She's going to slay me. I just know it.

Kentucky tugged at her sweater and caught it and her t-shirt in his fingers, dragging it up and over her head. He cupped her breasts and pinched first one nipple, then the other. "You have the most perfect tits. Perfect for my hands." He slid his hand down her torso, his fingers stroking along the edge of the leggings she was wearing.

"You are making me crazy."

"Crazy. I love you crazy." He repeated the featherlight touches. "If doing this drives you crazy," he pressed a kiss to her cheek, "maybe I should keep on doing it."

"You're teasing me." He chuckled softly against her ear, making her squirm and him want so much more. He wanted her needy, desperate, and… wet. God, he was so, so incredibly turned on right now.

"Tuck, I ache so much."

"I know, baby. I'm not just torturing you." He tugged at the waistband of her leggings with the tips of his fingers and growled in answer to her gasp at the arousal which built around them. Each and every single nerve ending he had hummed with pleasure. "I'm torturing myself, too. Because I want to know if you ache. If your pussy aches and clenches for me."

"Oh, God."

"You are fucking beautiful every day, but here in bed with me when you blush just like that, you make me want to come way before either of us wants that to happen," Kentucky praised her softly. His words may be crude, but even he could hear that, his voice tinged with a desperate need like he'd never felt before. He turned her head so he could kiss her. "Tell me you want this?" He held his breath for her answer. Because damn, if she said stop, it just might kill him to comply with her wishes. But he'd do it anyway.

"Yes," she whimpered. "Please. I want this. I want you. I want us."

That was all he needed to hear. Kentucky groaned and wasted no time pushing her leggings and panties down her thighs. Thankfully, she wiggled and helped him push them off completely. He drank in the needy whimpers with his lips. "God, I need you so much. I've dreamed of this so often since I left."

"I love that you did," she admitted softly. "Because I dreamed about you, too." There it was again, the blush he was coming to crave almost as much as he did his next breath.

"Someday I'm going to have you tell me what makes you blush that beautiful color of rose." Once she was completely naked, he ran his hand across her bare skin.

"Nobody told me that your touch would burn so hot. I didn't know that could happen."

He hadn't either until she'd touched him the first time. Her fingertips left a trail of fire along his arms. If he closed his eyes, even after all these months, he could still feel it. "I think it's an us thing," he said between kisses. "Because your touch does the same to me." He skimmed his hand down over her mound, dipped the tip of one finger into her slit, and stroked her.

"Yes," she cried out when he circled her clit with his calloused fingers.

The man who had waited for so long to hear her cry of pleasure thrilled at the sound. It was one he wanted to live in his memories. When her pussy clenched around his finger, he pressed his other hand against his dick, reminding himself that was not the time to be right at the edge of the bliss he knew was to come. "Jesus, Becky. You're so wet for me. I love it," he groaned and circled her opening with the pad of his finger.

She moved her hips and pressed down on his hand. "I need more, Kentucky. Please don't make me wait."

"I'm making both of us wait," Kentucky reminded her. He pressed and rubbed at her opening, not quite entering her. "How does that feel?"

"So good." She wiggled her hips, trying to get him to do… something. "I just need more, Tuck. Please." The last word came out as a full-on whine.

He rubbed his fingers up and down her slit, gathering up her juices and rubbing her clit as she moaned for him. "Beautiful, baby, so beautiful."

"I'm right there. So close." She shook under his touch. "So close." Becky squeezed her eyes shut and arched against him. "So close," she repeated, chanting the words. She clutched at the covers of the bed as if she needed something to hold onto.

He stroked up her body and tweaked a nipple, then pulled back, smiling when Becky gasped and growled in frustration. "Easy, love. I need to grab a condom."

"Yeah." She rolled over to watch him. "I've been tested every month since, but you need to wear a condom just in case…"

"Shh." He reached for his pants and fumbled for his wallet. Thankfully, he'd remembered to take it out of his go-bag on the way here. He was pretty sure that was still outside and Becky would probably kill him if he had to run outside buck ass naked to find it. Never mind what the owners would say, because that he wouldn't bear thinking about. He flipped open the wallet and grabbed the foil packet before dropping the pants and wallet back to the floor.

"Tuck?"

"Yes, baby?"

"Why does your condom packet have a chicken on it?"

"Huh?" He turned the condom over in his hand and squinted at it. "What the hell? Shit." He reached for his wallet again, flipping through the sections until he found the other foil packet. "This better not be a fucking ramen noodle seasoning packet, too, or I swear I'm taking us to town stark naked and the locals are gonna think we are into nudism or some shit."

She stared at him for a couple of seconds before laughter bubbled out of her. "This brings new meaning to spicy sex."

"That," he nodded to where he'd tossed the first packet, "will tell you the last time I needed a condom. I didn't even realize it was a seasoning package." He ripped open what better be a condom or his dick was going to be on fire, and not for a reason he wanted, and huffed out a relieved sigh when it was the latex he needed.

"Come here, lover boy, and give me all that spicy loving."

She howled with laughter and he couldn't help but chuckle along. He swiftly worked the condom onto his aching cock and went back to her. "You said spicy?"

"Mmh."

He captured her lips and kissed her deep, messy, and slow, and slid his hand down her thigh, gently lifting her leg and placing her foot on the bed, opening her up to him, giving him more access. Then he went back to stroking and circling over her clit until she was writhing under him. "That's it, so damn beautiful."

"Kentucky Smith, I swear if you don't..."

"Don't let you come, you'll murder me?" he finished for her.

"Yes... that," she replied, her voice a breathy whimper.

"I got you, baby." He carefully pushed one finger all the way inside her. "So tight." He kissed his way down from her collarbone to her right nipple and captured it with his mouth, sucking hard as she clenched around him. He moved his mouth to her other breast and nipped at it before licking and sucking away the sting. He needed her just on the edge of losing her mind, because once he got inside her, he already knew there was no way he would survive how her juices dripped and she clenched around him. He lavished love and attention on first one breast and then the other as he finger-fucked her in a steady rhythm.

"Baby." She smacked at his shoulder. "Pleaseee..."

"Bossy. My bossy Becky!" He ground the palm of his hand down on her little bundle of nerves, keeping her right on the edge of orgasm. "I don't want to hurt you, and I'm wide."

"I don't care." She tugged on his hair. "I need to feel the stretch and burn when you fuck me for real."

"Oh, baby, if you think this is fucking," he drawled out the words, "then I'm doing something wrong."

"Huh?"

"This is what making love is, doll face." He kept his fingers inside her pussy and leaned up to kiss first one cheek and then the other before he licked along the seam of her mouth. "Fucking is fast and furious. Between us, it will be hard and maybe against a wall. When we're in bed, we take our time. We love. We laugh and we make each other crazy until we can't wait any longer because the pure bliss is amplified, the stronger the need is between us." She rocked up against him as if she was trying to get his fingers deeper as she kissed him back, her fingernails digging into his shoulders as she clawed at him.

"I..."

He smiled and kissed her softly as he settled between her thighs. "Now you understand." He pushed one arm under her back and snaked around her waist, tilting her hips as his cock nudged at her entrance. "Ready?"

"Yesss."

He cupped her face with his other hand and stared into her eyes as he pushed into her in one slow, steady stroke.

"Oh." She breathed out the word on a sigh, her legs coming up to wrap around his waist, pushing on his ass, trying to get him to move faster. "More."

An intense pressure built low in his balls. His cock throbbed and ached with every clench as her muscles spasmed around him. He tightened his grip on her hips, pulling her toward him as he bottomed out inside her, her moan letting him know she was right there with him. "Baby," he groaned and pressed his lips to the spot where her shoulder met her neck before biting down gently on the same spot, just enough to sting.

"Move, do something."

"Becky," he warned. But she wouldn't let him wait a second, never mind a minute, so he could remind himself not to rush. She rolled her hips against him, and he cried out with overwhelming pleasure. When she rolled her hips again and sighed, a breathy sound of wonderment, any control he had left, got up and left the building. He gripped her hips with both hands, holding her in place for him, and drew his hips back until only the head of his cock stretched her opening. He waited until her closed eyelids lifted, and she watched him. Then he pushed in hard and fast, making her gasp. He repeated the move three times, then four before he couldn't take it anymore, and built up a steady rhythm.

"Tuck. Baby. Mmh. Yes. Tuck. More. Please."

Her words drove him onward, and he changed the angle of his thrusts, hitting a sensitive spot deep insider her. Becky's entire body spasmed and clenched around him, sending sparks of fire through his veins.

"Tuck," she moaned. "Tuck, please, I need…"

"Me," he growled the word. "You need me."

"Yes." He felt every one of her muscles tighten, and she

arched off the bed toward him as her orgasm ripped through her body. She clenched so tight around him, it almost hurt. But it was the look of rapture on her face which cracked open his soul and the love he felt for this lioness of a woman vibrated through him. "Becky," he ground out between clenched teeth as his cock pulsed and filled the condom inside her. She thrashed under him as they rode out their pleasure together. Until with a final, shuddering breath, the last of her orgasm released her, and she went limp under him. "Jesus. Baby…"

"Holy shit." Becky's whisper was barely audible as she gulped in air. She still trembled against him.

He gripped the base of the condom and carefully withdrew from her. He took care of the condom and dropped it into the trash can next to the bed. "Are you okay? Was that too much? Did I hurt–"

"Don't you dare finish that sentence." Her eyes stayed closed. "Don't you dare."

He gathered her into his arms and she curled around him. "Nope. I found some brain cells overseas and decided I better keep them." He kissed the side of her neck. "So I'm not gonna finish that sentence."

"Good." She snuggled into him, and within seconds her breathing had evened out, telling him she slept peacefully.

How in the hell did someone like me get so damn lucky to have someone like her in my world?

CHAPTER TWENTY-FIVE

Somehow, she knew what the buzzing of the phone on the counter meant before Kentucky even got off the couch to check it. They'd had almost two months of bliss, secluded here in the mountains. Spending their free time wandering around the lake and just enjoying being free. Becky hit mute on her computer screen and turned to look at him when he cleared his throat. "When do you leave?"

"Tomorrow at noon."

"Then we still have tonight." She refused to be the woman who begged him to stay, or the one who cried where he could see. She knew who he was. She understood his job better than most.

"Yes, baby. We still have tonight." He winked at her and waved her back to the computer. "I need to make some calls and stuff, but when you're finished for the day, we'll go out to eat. That okay?"

"Yes, Tuck, that's perfect." She had no choice but to go back to work. She had students waiting. "I'll be done in about half an hour."

"Awesome. I'll call the restaurant and book us a table."

Not that either of them thought the place would be booked out. At this time of year, a lot of tourists had cookouts near the lake or barbecues near whichever cabins they were staying in.

Becky blew out a breath and switched the microphone back on. "Sorry about that."

"No problem, Miss Becky. I finished all the questions."

"If you email them to me, I'll have them graded for you on Monday," she promised. "But you are doing awesome. Did you hear back from the school over here?"

"Yes. I have a phone interview in two months. Will you help me prepare?"

"Of course, I will." There was no way she'd let her student down. "If you let me know the dates, we'll schedule in some extra classes that week and we can do mock interviews."

"You're the best, Miss Becky. Thank you."

"Go on, have an awesome weekend." She waved to her student and hit end on the call. While it was awesome to not have to leave the house for work, sometimes figuring out a decent work life balance sucked. This week she'd over-stretched her limits and added two new students, both from a business back east who had brought staff across from Europe to fill a gap in their US branch. Meeting new people, even online, took a lot out of her. At the back of her mind, she was always aware that the people hunting her were still out there. It frustrated Kentucky so much that she'd taken to internalizing her fear as much as possible. He should be able to enjoy the times when he didn't have to go to work. And he didn't need to be worrying about her when he left. If worrying about her distracted him and someone got hurt, he'd never forgive himself, and possibly not her either.

"Babe, they only have a table for seven." Kentucky stuck his head in the door. "As soon as you are ready, we can go."

"I need ten minutes to change out of my jammie pants."

What she wore on her bottom half didn't matter when she was sitting at a computer. She did normally attempt to look presentable on her top half though, and today she wore a blue blouse which Kentucky insisted she needed as it made her eyes a beautiful shade of aqua. Who was she to try to tell him she didn't need clothes? She still didn't have half her stuff from San Diego, although the girls had promised to visit and bring everything up soon. Having her own things would be so awesome, and seeing the other women even more so.

She swiftly pulled off her jammie pants and pulled on a pair of dark wash jeans. After tucking the blouse into the waistband, she added a belt and grabbed a clean sweater to put over her shoulders. The nights could get chilly up here, and every time she forgot to bring her own sweater, she ended up wearing Kentucky's. After pulling on a pair of low-heeled boots and brushing out her hair, she almost called it good, but went back to the mirror to add some mascara and lip gloss. "There, that will do."

"I'm thinking I might have changed my mind about eating dinner out." The leer in Kentucky's voice made her press her thighs together. Her body knew exactly what that tone offered. Blissed out orgasms, which made her weak at the knees.

"Nuh—uh." As much as she loved blissed out orgasms which made her weak at the knees, he needed to have a decent meal before he left in the morning, and they had exactly zero food in the fridge because neither of them had wanted to go to the store earlier. "We go eat first," she told him. "Then you get to do the rest."

"Deal. What are you waiting for, woman? Move that pretty booty, we have plans when we get home."

If someone had told her when she'd met him that Kentucky Smith was a huge kid at heart, she'd have laughed straight in their faces. Now she saw the heart inside the man, and she couldn't deny it any longer, not even to herself. She loved him. Loved everything about him. Now she just had to figure out how to tell him.

And hope it doesn't send him running for the hills.

Not gonna happen.

It might.

And this right here was why she hadn't told him yet. Everyone and everything she'd ever loved had either left her or thrown her away. She was so afraid to risk the same happening with him. Losing him would not only destroy what was left of her heart, but it would also destroy any promise she had of a happy future. Because a future without Kentucky in it would never, ever be happy.

Walking into the restaurant, she spotted Summer. She was just about to walk over there and say hello when she saw who she was sitting with. "Tuck, look." She nudged him with her elbow. "Isn't that Mozart?"

"Yeah." He gave a chin lift to his friend. "When I spoke to Cookie earlier, he said Mozart was up here this week." There was a weird tone to his voice, but she didn't have time to figure out what caused it as Kentucky cocked his head to one side and asked, "Is that your friend Summer?"

She nodded.

"Want to go over and say hello?"

Yes. I want to know how they know each other and what's going on.

"No, Tuck." As curious as she was, they had other plans. "Tonight is for us. I want to spend every second we have with just us. Is that selfish?"

"No," Kentucky replied. "Not if I feel exactly the same way." He placed his hand on the small of her back in that move she loved so much and guided her toward their table. When she slid into her seat, he leaned down and brushed a kiss against her temple. "Did I tell you how beautiful you look tonight?"

Just like that, the world faded away and everything around them disappeared. Tonight was for them. The bad guys could wait until morning when she had to face him leaving again. But for now, all was finally right in her world.

* * *

Becky glanced at the clock. She had another hour and a half before she had to log in for her lesson. She switched on the kettle and rummaged in the fridge for something to eat. "Thankfully, Tuck can't see that I haven't been to the store yet." He'd been gone three days, and she hadn't ventured out of the cabin since.

You're moping.

I am not.

Yes... totally moping.

Her internal arguing was cut off by a knock at the door. She glanced from the open fridge to the closed front door and back again. When the knocking sounded again, she sighed and kicked the fridge door shut. "I'm so totally going to boot his ass when he comes back." Mrs. Zorastrian had been hovering and had checked up on her so many times since Kentucky had left that she just knew he'd asked her to keep an eye on her. "As if I don't know how to look after myself." Muttering, she went to answer the door. "I swear I am okay, Mrs. Zor—" Her eyes widened in shock when she realized it wasn't her landlady who stood there.

"I don't know who Mrs. Zor is." Caroline grinned at her. "But I'm sure she'll be thrilled to know you are okay. I am, too."

Becky reached for the other woman and squished her into a hug. "What are you doing here? Come in."

"Can we come in, too?"

"OMG!" she squealed in excitement. "Fee, Al'Bama." She didn't know why they were here. She was just thrilled they were.

"We are on our way to do a favor for Mozart," Caroline explained as she dragged them into the cabin. "And we wanted to see if you want to come along, too."

"Eeep. He's serious about Summer!" She didn't bother to phrase it as a question. She already knew the answer. She remembered how he'd looked at her friend at the restaurant the other night.

"Yes, he is." Caroline dropped her purse on the couch. "Help me empty the truck. We have your things. The guys grabbed them from Mozart's house last week."

"You seriously brought them here?" She followed them back out to the car.

"Well, it's only clothes and books. I want to read your Riley Edwards series, if you don't mind lending them to me."

"You are a Riley fan? How did I not know this?"

"We all are," Fiona chimed in. "And you have all the Blue Team books. If you'll lend them to us, we promise we'll be careful."

She grabbed the suitcase Caroline put on the ground, "If it was anyone else asking, I'd say no."

"And none of us would blame you." Fiona nodded to a bag on the back seat of Caroline's car. "Those are the books."

"If you want to read them, Tuck said we'd be down in San Diego after he gets back, and I can pick them up then," she offered. "I just don't know if he'll be back tomorrow, next week, or next month."

"We all feel that in our souls," Alabama said. "Ours are working, too."

"Damn."

"We're used to it." They lugged all her belongings into the

cabin. "Do you mind if I use your bathroom? I've been in the car too long, I think."

"Not at all." She pointed past the stairs. "It's just through there."

"So can you come visit Summer with us?"

"I have to work this afternoon," she explained. "But how about I meet you guys for dinner and then we can all stay at one place and visit some more?"

"That totally works." Fiona hugged her. "I don't know how to thank you for getting me and Alabama to bake cookies with you at Christmas. We needed that more than you know."

"So did I, sister. So did I." She glanced at the clock on the wall. "My lesson starts in ten minutes. I'm sorry. I wish I could just cancel it. Let me see if I can try…"

"Hey." Caroline patted her arm. "It's okay. We'll see you for dinner tonight. We're the ones who just showed up with no notice at all and totally understand that you have to work. Walk us out, hug us, and we'll see you when you're finished with work."

"Working is overrated," she grumbled and did as Caroline had asked. By the time the girls had been hugged and loaded back into the car, she was down to two minutes to the start of her class. Yet she still waited until their car disappeared from view before she turned and went back into the cabin and shut the door behind her.

"Hello, Becky. Remember me?"

CHAPTER TWENTY-SIX

The second the phone rang with the ringtone he recognized, Tex hit answer. "Hey, Ice. You ladies okay? Or do I need to come down there loaded for bear?"

"Bear. Bring bear." Caroline's voice was clipped and filled with fear. "We need all the bear you've got."

"What's wrong?"

"We went to Big Bear Lake to meet Mozart's Summer..."

Shit, had something happened to Summer? Mozart was going to lose his ever-loving mind. "Go on." He knew Caroline well enough to know she needed to do things in a way that made logical sense to her.

"We brought Becky up everything she'd left in San Diego," Caroline explained. "She was meant to meet us for dinner and didn't answer her phone when we called to check on her. But I thought maybe Kentucky had come home because she wasn't there."

Tex was already logging into the cameras, which had been set up by Caleb when Kentucky and Becky had rented the cabin. He shot off a message to Trev just in case there was any intel he wasn't aware of.

"The door was wide open, and everything scattered about." Caroline broke down in tears, and Tex had a hard time understanding what she was saying.

"Why didn't she go to with you when you went to see Summer?"

"She had an online lesson to give..."

It can't be that easy. That easy never happens in my world.

"I'm looking, Ice. I swear I'm looking," he reassured her as he logged into the account he'd set up for Becky and prayed to every god he could think of and a few he was pretty sure he'd made up in his head.

Please let there be something there.

He clicked through the folders until he found the one for today's lesson. "I've got something, Ice. I need to call Nemesis and get Kentucky and the guys back, stat."

"Okay. Please find her." Caroline sniffed and ended the call.

Tex's mouse hovered over the lesson recording, and he blew out a slow breath before he hit play. Becky's face immediately filled the screen.

"Hello, Becky. Remember me?"

He hit pause on the playback and scribbled down the word *male* on his notepad and *known to her,* then hit play again. On the screen, Becky whirled around and threw something, making the man grunt, then she bolted out of view.

Fuck!

There it was—confirmation this wasn't an old friend coming to visit. People, and especially women like Becky, didn't run like that if they were pleased to see someone. That version of events would involve squeals, wine, and a hell of a lot of hugs. At least in his experience. He tapped out the number for Nemesis Inc.

"I need your war room, stat." He didn't even wait for the

woman who answered the phone to finish her greeting. "Tell Trev that John Keegan is on the phone and we have a situation that's TARFU level whacked. He'll know what I mean."

"Yes, sir. One moment, please."

Clearly, she understood that Things Are Really Fucked Up and he needed to talk to Trev immediately.

"What's doing, Tex?" Trev came on the line, cutting off the hold music.

"You didn't see my message, did you?" He didn't bother waiting for an answer, but forged on ahead. "Smith's woman was kidnapped from Big Bear Lake. I need him back and a team on the ground there, stat."

"Fuck. On it. Find out what you can. I'll be back in a sec." The infuriating hold music came back on in his ear and Tex put the phone on loudspeaker while he went back to watching—or rather, listening to—what was happening on the Zoom recording.

From the shape of the person who ran past the screen and the voice, he knew whoever was there with Becky was a man. He could hear a scuffle and a howl of rage. "Good girl." He was so damn proud of her. She was fighting back. But then Becky yelped, and silence filtered through the speakers. "Damn." Then the recording flickered, splitting the screen in two, revealing Becky's student turning up for her lesson.

"Tex?"

"Yeah, still here," he answered Trev. "I can't see jack on the screen. A man spoke, she threw something, then took off running. There was a scuffle, and now nothing."

"I've got them on the outdoor cameras," Trev growled. Clearly, he wasn't at all pleased by what he was looking at. "They are in her car. That's one your guys organized. Can you track it?"

"Yeah. Gimme five."

"Thanks. Nemesis is on the phone to Kentucky. He's

gonna be coming in hot and mad in a couple of hours as they were down in Colombia. They're jumping a bird in about ten minutes."

"Copy that."

* * *

KENTUCKY PUNCHED the pillow and settled back into it. It was too fucking hot and humid to sleep. But after being the one away on watch for over twenty-four hours, he couldn't put it off anymore. His eyeballs hurt with the need for darkness and sleep. He rubbed them with the back of his hands and pulled the thin sheet over his head, hoping sleep would come fast. He was just about at that point where you were drifting between wakefulness and sleep when someone hammered on the door. "Fucking hell," he muttered before shouting, "Yeah?"

"Yo, Ken. Boss wants you on the phone, stat."

Dalton's timing was fucking epic as always. He must have heard him rolling down the fucking shutters. "Damn." Grumbling, he threw back the covers. "Coming." He pulled on his combat pants but didn't bother to button them. Everyone on his team was male, and if any of them had a fucking issue with some skin showing, then they could shut their freaking eyes. "What's wrong?"

"No clue."

He took the 'family emergency' phone Tate handed him, his stomach clenching as angry wasps warned him what was coming next was going to suck. "Kentucky here."

"Ken, get your ass to the coordinates I'm sending to this phone. Wrap everything up," Dalton ordered. "That fucker isn't our problem anymore. We have bigger fish to fry."

"Excuse me?" This didn't make sense. If they had been called off the job of staking out this drug king pin's property in the hopes he'd show his face, then Dalton would have used the normal channels of communication to inform them of such. "Spill it, Boss. What aren't you telling me?"

Dalton's huff was audible. Clearly, he didn't want to say whatever it was needed saying. Kentucky leaned his ass against the wall, knowing he would probably need it for support when the blow fell, and asked the first logical question which popped into his mind. "My mother?"

"No..." Dalton's voice trailed off.

He knew. He just knew.

Fuck. No. No. No. Not my Becky.

He'd been an idiot to leave her unprotected. He should have insisted she go to the ranch, where she'd be fucking safe. Now she was gone and there wasn't a damn thing he could do about it but blame himself. "What happened?"

"We aren't sure yet," Dalton admitted. "All we know for sure is she's missing, and Trev and Keegan are working on it. I've pulled all resources and have all available teams on their way there."

He had to work hard to keep himself from dropping to the floor and even harder to keep his voice even. "Explain."

Dalton either ignored his question or didn't answer it on purpose as he spoke right over him. "Pack your shit and get to the rendezvous point. One of the McKinnon brothers is giving you a ride to the Garrett Ranch in Texas. From there I'll have a bird waiting for you to get you to California."

He could picture Dalton pacing around, either in his office or the war room depending on where he was making this call. "I have one question." He paused. "Well, two."

"Hit me."

"Am I sanctioned to kill this motherfucker?"

"Yes, and the second?"

"What's his fucking name?"

"We're working on that bit," Dalton advised. "Make sure

you don't miss the rendezvous with McKinnon. We'll find your girl."

"Whoa. Back up. Wait… wait." His brain struggled with the change in direction this conversation was going. This phone was only ever used for deaths in the family. He sucked in a breath, not daring to hope he'd understood wrong, and choked out the words, "She's not dead?"

"Bro, hell no… no, she's not dead."

Relief slammed into him so hard that this time he dropped to his knees. Not dead meant she was still breathing. If his Becky was alive, then he was coming for her. Everyone and anyone involved better get the hell out of his way. Period.

"At least we have no evidence of that," Dalton corrected. "She's missing. Kidnapped. And we are going to get her back. Alive! Do you hear me, Smith? Get your shit together," he ordered. "That's a fucking order."

"Yeah."

"Do you fucking understand me, Smith?" Dalton demanded. "We will get your woman back, and we will take out the fucker who had her and make sure this doesn't happen again."

"Roger that." He snapped his fingers, not that he needed to get the guys' attention, as they were all focused on him. They weren't even trying to be covert about it. "We'll be outta here in less than ten."

"Good," Dalton replied. "I've gotta go. Because Spider has orders to not wait for anyone, even me, on this one, and I still need to make it to the airstrip."

Holy shit, even Dalton was coming. He hadn't left the ranch since Lina had given birth. "Thanks, Boss, I appreciate—"

"Don't you dare finish that fucking sentence. Move your ass. Time's a wasting."

"Yes, sir." He hit end on the call. "We're leaving. My Becky is missing." Nothing else was needed, the guys exploded into action, packing gear and everything which couldn't be left behind. When Kentucky climbed into the truck, he glanced at his watch. It had taken them exactly seven minutes from the time he ended the call and him starting the engine.

I'm coming, doll face. Hold on for me. You just gotta hold on until I come for you.

CHAPTER TWENTY-SEVEN

Becky jerked awake and screamed behind the tape covering her mouth. Pain radiated from her arms and legs where they stretched, tied between the bars of the cage she'd been pushed into.

No. No. No. No.

This can't be happening again. It just can't.

Wake up. Wake up. Wake up.

"I don't think our Becky likes her new accommodations, Jimmy," a voice straight out of her nightmares sneered. "She should be grateful you didn't kill her for stabbing you."

"I still think we should kill the bitch," Jimmy whined. "She stabbed me. I didn't do nothin' but ask her if she'd missed me."

"We don't have orders to kill her," the first man said. "We are to bring her to the big boss, because he wants to know about that ranch, remember?"

Ranch?

Why couldn't she focus? What ranch? She didn't have a ranch. She hadn't lived on a ranch in months… Her head hurt so much. She didn't dare try to shake it again. The last time she'd fainted from the pain. When what they were saying eventually started to make sense to her, instead of being terrifying, it lit a spark of hope as it reminded her of the day she'd won her freedom before. She'd survived the first time. She'd survive this time. Because this time she *did* have someone waiting for her. Kentucky.

Oh my God.

If they thought she was able to tell them anything about the ranch in Montana, then they were in for one hell of a surprise, as she knew nothing about it. Even if she did, she wouldn't tell them.

Channel Willow. Be a Willow. Remember how she was when she was taken? Kentucky will come for you. Just as Cormack came for her.

Be a Willow.

Kentucky will come.

Tuck will come.

"SHE LOOKS RATHER FETCHING in that bikini, don't she?" Jimmy asked his partner.

"That's not a bikini, it's her bra and… you know what, never mind. It covers about the same as a bikini, so call it what you want."

At least she wasn't naked yet. She'd take it. She closed her eyes and let her head drop forward. Maybe if they thought she'd fainted again, they'd leave her alone. She didn't need their vulgar voices to remind her of what lay ahead.

He'll come.

Kentucky will come.

Maybe if she repeated it enough in her head, she'd believe it. Kentucky was working, she didn't even know what country he was in or when he'd be back. But he would come. She had to believe that. He would come for her.

She heard footsteps and a door opening and then closing again. But she didn't dare open her eyes or give any indication she was awake. They'd played these tricks before. If they knew she was awake… then it didn't bear thinking of. Slowly, while trying to ignore the pain in her joints from being strung up like a starfish, she drifted off to unconsciousness. Hours and minutes became a blur of pain, hunger, and nothingness. She had no concept of time or even where she was or if there was anyone else with her. Maybe it was better this way. This way, they weren't forcing her to do other things.

Tuck will come. He will come for me.

Tex or Trev will find me and Tuck will come.

She repeated the mantra in her head over and over. Despite everything and anything they taunted her with, nothing else registered except for the pain of her limbs being held in one position for so long and variations of…

Tuck will come for me.

She had no clue how long she'd been there when the pain in her arms went from dull—almost able to ignore it if she didn't move it—to excruciating. Finally, free of her bonds, she slumped forward, screaming in agony as her swollen body tried to readjust itself. Men's voices laughed as hands ruthlessly pulled her arms behind her back and tied them in that position, with no care for how much pain it caused her.

"Wh—?"

But she didn't have time to finish her sentence when a foul-tasting cloth was stuffed in her mouth and tape put over it. She gagged and choked against it.

Don't puke. Don't puke.

A rough cloth was pulled over her head and some asshole pushed at her legs, tying her ankles to her wrists as if she was a damn cow they needed to hogtie. With her eyelids swollen shut, she couldn't see, and no matter how much she struggled, her efforts were feeble at best against them both. And between them, they carried her somewhere and tossed her into something. She considered it a blessing that she passed out from the pain of the impact.

CHAPTER TWENTY-EIGHT

"TOC, Bravo One." Kentucky barely waited to have his comms device fully in his ear, or even his ass on the seat of the Blackhawk that Dalton had managed to either borrow or steal from somewhere before he connected with Trev. "Tell me you've got something. Did you find her?"

"Bravo One, TOC 2," Tex's voice replied. Clearly, he, too, had been patched in on this job. "You can bet your ass we did."

Kentucky didn't care about the logistics of it or how many rules or laws had been broken to have Tex on board. He only cared that he was. "Is she alive?" Everything else he could work with. But he needed her to be breathing… the alternative didn't bear thinking about. He strapped himself into his seat and tried to ignore the hesitation before Tex replied.

"As far as I can tell, yes," Tex replied. "Your assholes on this occasion are the Richards brothers. Johnny and Jimmy, aka Johnny and Jimmy Dick."

"I couldn't have picked more fitting names if I'd tried." He braced his feet in front of him and took the weapon Dalton handed him, cleared it, loaded it, and laid it across his knees. He nodded in response to Dalton's hand on his shoulder, silently asking if he was good. 'Good' was relative in this situation. "Ask me later tonight." He knew he was being short, and his voice clipped, but he figured if anyone understood why he didn't elaborate, it would be Dalton.

"Yeah." Dalton squeezed his shoulder with one hand, his other one braced against the roof of the Blackhawk, keeping him steady as it swooped to one side.

"Agreed. The Dickwad brothers have rap sheets as long as both of our arms," Tex said. "Jimmy Dick somehow managed to escape or evade capture in Billings. He not only has a grudge against your woman, but a debt to pay to The Organization. Our best guess is King threw a shit fit that yours and Jeep's women escaped him, and he wants them to fix it."

That was what he thought, too. "Just put me down anywhere within ten miles of those fuckers and they'll figure out pretty fast that the Royal Cock-bag is the least of their worries."

"We're working on it, buddy, we're working on it," Tex said. "Now flip to normal channels so we can get this show on the road."

"Roger that." He leaned his head back and shut his eyes, slowly working on pushing back everything inside him which made him the man whose woman was missing. Closing off his fears, his heart, and forcing his mind into warrior mode.

"TOC, ALL STATIONS."

Trev's call into his ear was louder than he expected, and he jumped and tensed as he waited for the update.

Damn, I'm edgy.

No shit, sherlock.

Across from Kentucky, Dalton thumbed his comms. "Go ahead, TOC."

"Sir, I just got a hit on facial recon," Trev informed them. "TOC Two agrees. It's both our dicks, and they're moving."

Someone further back in the helo snickered, and Dalton snapped his fingers, then drew one finger across his neck, informing whichever jackass it was to shut the fuck up.

"Where?"

"Straight down 1-25," Trev said. "They can't be stupid enough to make another run for Ramona airstrip, can they?"

"Boss, I'm flying right over 1-25 now," the pilot called. "Gimme a description, and let's see if we can find these mofos and give them a little heart attack."

"We're looking for a black 2019 Ford F-250 Super Duty King Ranch," Trev said. "Headed east on I-25."

This was going to be like looking for a needle in a haystack.

"I have a good news/bad news situation," Tex interrupted. "I'm tapped into some of the county's police scanners and there are reports of a similar truck with a sack in the bed, which appears to be trying to jump out of the bed. A concerned citizen called it in and dispatch has sent a patrol car to look. GPS is coming your way now."

"On it." The helo swooped off to the left before the pilot had even finished speaking. "Hold on to your hats and jocks, grandpas, because we're going fast."

"Jesus, if she jumps…"

"Shut it." He glared at Draven. He didn't need to think of what-ifs or maybes—she had to be okay. There was no other option.

"Sorry."

"I got them," the pilot called.

"Kinda hard to miss them with that patrol car flashing all those blues and twos," Dalton agreed.

"Want me to land right in front of his ass?"

"Can you hover?" Dalton asked. "Not quite land, I don't want to be sitting ducks."

Kentucky listened to the conversations going on around him but focused on one single goal. Get to Becky and get her safe. He felt the helo descending and unclipped the straps which held him in place.

"All Stations, TOC Two," Tex called. "I've let dispatch know we are stopping that truck and why. They are aware you are coming in and armed."

"Roger." Dalton moved next to the door and put his hand on the latch. Kentucky stacked up right on his ass with the others ready to roll behind him. "When the pilot calls it, we move on my count."

"Copy."

"I can't drift this bird backward for long," the pilot warned. "If they keep moving, I'm gonna have to circle around. I'm nose to nose with him now and he's still going."

"Go around and hover right over him," Dalton ordered. "We'll drop right on top of him."

"Roger." The Blackhawk swooped off and circled around. "On target."

Dalton ripped open the door. "Go. Go. Go."

Kentucky wasn't waiting to be told twice. He bolted for the door, jumped, and braced for impact. Thankfully, he didn't miss and landed directly on the bed of the truck. He scrambled on his hands and knees to where someone or something flopped about in a closed jute bag. "Becky? Doll face? I got you." He wrapped his arms around the bag and pulled it into his chest, rolling them out of the way as Dalton, followed by Jeep, landed almost on top of them.

Please be her. Please be her.

As Dalton went one way and Jeep the other, climbing over the roof of the truck and ripping open doors, they slid into the rear seats of the crew cab with weapons drawn.

Kentucky drew his blade and carefully cut the bag open while keeping his own body between it and the front of the truck.

"I got you. I got you, Becky." Relief slammed into him before he'd uncovered her face when he recognized the mole just below her colorbone. She'd bucked and fought him every inch of the way.

Fucking bastards.

"Boss, kill those fuckers before I do. They've taped her mouth and eyes shut." Rage warred with fear. But the more she struggled, the fear lowered, and he wrapped himself around her. He didn't dare try to remove the tape, not with the vehicle swerving all over the damn road. "I got you. I got you. You're safe, love. I'm here."

* * *

"I GOT YOU. I got you. You're safe, love. I'm here."

"I got you. I got you. You're safe, love. I'm here."

"I got you. I got you. You're safe, love. I'm here."

It took a hot minute for the words to make sense and a few minutes more to recognize the feel of the arms. Behind her gag, she screamed his name, but it came out muffled and butchered. "Rucky."

"I got you. I got you. You're safe, love. I'm here," he crooned in her ear. She stopped struggling when he wrapped himself tighter around her. This time she welcomed the pain, it allowed her to stay awake and focus on his voice. "You came. You came." Not that he'd be able to understand her, but she kept trying to say the words anyway.

"I'm gonna try and get this tape off your mouth, doll face. This is gonna hurt."

"Yash, pees. Off." She could barely breathe through her stuffed-up nose. He could rip her lips off at this point, and she'd be grateful. She felt whatever vehicle they were in shudder to a stop, and only Kentucky's hold on her kept her in place.

"Medic, I need a medic, stat!" Kentucky yelled. "Get me a fucking medic, stat."

It couldn't be that bad. She had some tape on her face. Even her hands and legs didn't hurt anymore.

"Here, sir, let me through."

She didn't recognize the voices and shrunk away from them as much as she could, given the circumstances.

"It's okay, baby, I got you," Kentucky crooned in her ear. "I'm not leaving. I'm just making some room for the ambulance guys, okay? They can help you better than me."

She could feel the first responders assessing her, and tried not to flinch away every time they touched her. But she couldn't help herself, only Kentucky's voice kept her from screaming and trying to run away.

"This may pinch."

Ouch. Ow. Ow. Fuck, that hurts. Oh my God, that hurts.

Pain radiated from her fingertips and all the way through her body. She screamed behind the gag and blackness descended, bringing blessed relief from the pain.

CHAPTER TWENTY-NINE

Four days. For four long hellish days, they'd kept Becky sedated as they'd worked to save her hands and feet. Having the circulation almost cut off for so long had caused more issues than the doctors would have liked. Kentucky was going out of his mind. Did they not realize how much he needed her? Without Becky, he struggled to breathe, never mind function.

"Like I said, Mr. Smith, your fiancée is probably going to have nerve damage. We don't know how long it will take to repair itself..."

"I don't need to know how long it will take," Kentucky interrupted. "I just need to know that she's going to be okay."

"Like I said, we don't know...."

"Then get me someone who does know." He was so over this shit of people talking in circles and with medical speak. Why the hell couldn't they just tell him what it meant in plain freaking English? "I don't care what it costs, or that she has no insurance. I'll pay for it myself. Get someone..."

"Tuck..."

He whirled around at the first croak from behind him.

That scratchy whispered sound, the sweetest music he'd ever heard in his life. "Becky?" He shot across the room to her bedside and grabbed her hand, leaning over her. If she saw or felt the tears dripping down his face, he didn't care. They would tell her how scared he'd been for her.

"Stop yelling," she whispered. "My head hurts."

"Shh, don't talk. How are you feeling?"

Idiot, first you tell her not to talk. Then you ask her a question. Jeez. Get a grip.

"Dopey. Hurts."

"Mr. Smith, you have to move," the doctor he'd been talking to insisted. "I need to check my patient."

"I'll stay out of your way." He'd learned his lesson the last time Dalton and Jeep had been called to haul his ass out of the room. "I won't make trouble. Just please don't make me leave her."

"The first time you are in my way or you compromise her safety, then you are out of here."

He could deal with that. He wound his fingers into hers and moved back a step to allow the doctor close enough to check her. This he could deal with. But when they threw him out, that was what caused a problem. "I'll behave. I promise." He squeezed Becky's fingers lightly when she snorted. She was alive. She was awake. She was talking. He'd take it.

By the time the doctor and nurses were done, Becky had drifted off to sleep. He squeezed his eyes shut. Fuck, he wanted her to know he was here. He wasn't leaving. Staring down at their joined hands, all he could do was stand there here and hope like hell he wasn't hurting her. He pressed a kiss to the back of her hand. "I'll just stand here until you wake up."

"No need to do that, Mr. Smith." A nurse picked up the chair he'd spent the last four days in and moved it behind him. "I'll help you sit so you can be close to her."

"Thank you."

"If my man was like that with me," the nurse guided him into the chair, "I'd want him to be comfortable, too." She patted his shoulder. "Hit the call button if you need anything."

"Thank you, Ma'am." He leaned his head on the bed near Becky's hand and closed his eyes. He just needed a minute to find his strength again. Just a minute to rest while she did.

Becky, pulling her hand free of his, woke him, and his eyes jerked open. Her fingers skimmed up his shoulder and carded through his hair. "Hi."

"Hi, baby," he whispered softly. He didn't need the nurses to pile in here just yet. He needed a minute for just them before they were surrounded by people. "How are you feeling?"

"So tired."

"I love you." There was no way he was letting a second longer go by before making her understand what she meant to him. "I swear I love you."

Tears rolled down her face, and she smiled at him. "I love you, too. I knew you would come for me. That's how I knew... how I knew you loved me and I loved you. Because I didn't doubt you would come."

"I'll always come for you. I don't care if I'm old, gray, and am running a Zimmer frame instead of a Blackhawk, but I'll always come."

"I know."

Thank fuck! His biggest fear was losing her. His second, that she didn't know she was no longer alone. "Becky?"

"Hmm."

"Will you marry me?" This probably wasn't the most ideal time. It definitely wasn't the most ideal place. But they were the right words, and they came right from his heart. "Please say you will marry me." Her hand stilled in his hair, and he braced himself for what she would say next.

"I can't have children. Every man deserves children, especially you."

She still didn't understand. Nothing else mattered but having her in his life, as his wife. His forever. "I don't care." He would make her understand. "Please marry me anyway. If we decide children are something *we*, not me, *we*, want at some point, then we can adopt or foster," he promised. "Blood doesn't make a family… love does."

"But they wouldn't be yours."

"No, they would be ours. Chosen family." While she was considering his words, he started coming up with other ways to convince her he didn't need children. Sure, they'd be awesome if it happened for them. But he needed her. Children he could live without. Her… he absolutely couldn't.

"Yes, but only if…" She paused and swiped a tear away. "Your momma helps organize it. Because I wouldn't know how to."

"Deal." He carefully scooped her into his arms. "My mom will be thrilled to help you do it."

Bring it on, life. Let's dance because with Becky at my side, I can do anything. This time we win and we get the fairy tale.

"I love you, Becky."

"I love you, too, Tuck."

EPILOGUE

NEMESIS RANCH—6 MONTHS LATER.

Draven pulled at the bow tie and tugged it free of his neck. He'd never understand why weddings required bow ties and monkey suits. "Fucking torture devices." He flopped into one of the chairs surrounding the firepit. Kentucky and Becky were married. The speeches were done. The food eaten. The first dance done. Momma Smith had cried, smiled, and insisted Kentucky's father would have been so proud of him and delighted to have Becky in the family.

Who the hell knew Tex Keegan would scrub up so well, although if Draven was to hazard a guess, the bridesmaids, aka Caroline Steel and her posse from California, had a little something to do with that. He snorted a laugh when he remembered how tiny Willow Ford had squared up to Kentucky and warned him, he better not make Becky cry or she'd be whipping out some of her daddy's old tricks and making his life hell for at least a decade. Nope, weddings and shit weren't for him. He was happy for his friends. But that happily ever after shit wasn't in his wheelhouse.

As if fate had been waiting for him to toss her a challenge, his phone buzzed and beeped in his ass pocket. This better not be someone wanting him to do anything. He had exactly zero plans for the next month but to sleep, eat, maybe drink some beers, before repeating everything all over again. He pulled out the phone and scowled at the screen. The notification had already disappeared from the screen. Of course, it had. Why wouldn't it disappear, forcing him to remember his password? He was down to last chance saloon on the password front when he finally got it right and his phone unlocked.

IF: 4°30'17.99"S - 21°42'52.89"E

He stared at the coordinates for a heartbeat until his brain figured out what they were and who had sent them. "Shit."

DK: On my way.

If there was ever going to be a person, besides the ones on this ranch tonight, who he would come on the run with no questions asked for, it was this woman. His childhood friend. "What kind of shit have you gotten yourself into now, brat?" He drained the glass of brandy and turned in time to see Kentucky kissing his bride as he carried her over the threshold of their newly built cabin. "Have the best life," he whispered softly. "You both earned it."

He waited until the door had closed behind them before he went looking for Trev. If he put those coordinates into google maps, he'd probably end up in the fucking Congo or somewhere and that wouldn't help the little troublemaker who loved to make him batshit.

He made his way through everyone, sidestepped to avoid stepping on Mozart's woman's toes as he made his way to where Trev was propping up the bar with a dark scowl on his face. He hadn't even known Mozart had a woman, but Summer Pack was one hell of a strong lady, that she'd been through a similar situation to Becky and Willow, made her an ideal match for Sam Reed. He tapped Trev on the shoulder. "What's wrong, bro? This is meant to be a happy day.

What have you got to look like you want to punch someone for?"

"I think I have hives." Trev tipped his beer bottle toward the dance floor and shuddered. "Kentucky's momma made me dance."

"What's wrong with that?"

"I don't dance."

He wasn't above needling him a little bit. "Apparently Ma Smith thinks you do." When Trev's face darkened, he remembered he needed him on his side. "Wanna get out of here and classify it as work?"

"Hell yes." Trev placed his beer bottle on the bar. "What did you do?"

"Nope," he shook his head, "it's not me this time. It's a friend of mine. She sent me coordinates, and I need to be sure I head in the right direction."

"She?" He could hear the curiosity in Trev's voice, but figured he didn't need to tell him everything. Especially the bits which were none of his business.

"My little sister's friend from when we were kids."

"Bro." Trev walked beside him as they made it to the door which led to the main offices. He punched in the code to open it for them. "Have you not watched the Hallmark movies… sister's best friend is in trouble and you run in to save the day. Do I say congratulations now, or should I wait until you figure it out?"

"Are you drunk?" Trev better not be so drunk he couldn't figure out how to switch on his computers. "I'm just going to save her butt and drop her home. It's not anything weird or wonderful."

"If you say so…."

"She is a child, Trev. A kid! What the hell do you think I am?"

"How old is your 'little' sister, bro?" Trev pulled back his chair, sat in it, and scooted forward until he was in front of his keyboard.

"What's that got to do with anything?"

"You said the person who sent you the message is a child. Is your sister also a child?"

Oh, he could just go fuck himself sideways with a dry cactus, preferably in the ass. "Man, you aren't even barking in the same forest, never mind at the same fucking tree." He pulled out his phone and handed it to him. "It's the last message."

Trev sighed and unlocked his computer. "So you haven't been bitten by the love bug then?"

"Hell no, I just need to go grab India and make sure my sister isn't right there beside her causing chaos or my mom's going to lose her shit. Where am I going?"

"Um. Gimme a sec." Trev tapped the coordinates into his program and they both watched as it zoomed in on a location. "You, bro, are heading to The DRC."

BOOKS BY BELLA STONE

Nemesis Inc. Bravo Team

Rexar

Kentucky

NEMESIS INC: ALPHA TEAM

Dalton

Cormack

Logan

Rory

ABOUT THE AUTHOR

Bella Stone is the MF Pen name for Annabella Stone, all books published under this name will be MF. While there may be character crossover to my Annabella stories, the storylines etc. will be different to the story arcs in Panthers, Tags of Honor, etc.

Newsletter/Free book: https://BookHip.com/CTQKFRD
Facebook: https://www.facebook.com/authorbellastone
Website: https://www.annabellastone.com/bella-stone

Annabella Stone and Bella Stone are the alter egos of a wife and mom, who was lucky enough to find happy ever after with her own personal hero.
Annabella loves to write Military Romance and Romantic Suspense where warriors love harder when bullets fly. She believes in love at first sight and wants everyone to have the happy ever they deserve. Even if they have to dodge bullets and fight with everything that they are to get it.
Born and raised in Ireland, Annabella has a Grá for a good story and the breakfast blaa, but funnily enough, prefers Jack Daniels to Irish whiskey. Having lived across 7 countries and 3 continents over the last thirty years, she loves to explore new places and cultures. In her world, coffee is king, and she is 100% sure it deserves it's own food group.
Annabella is owned by a pack of malamutes, whom she loves to both work and show. If you can't find her at the computer writing, chances are she and her woofers have escaped to

enjoy at day at a dog show, or they are on a mountain trail with the dryland rig or the sled, depending on the time of year.

Annabella's motto is "Live life like a malamute who found the gate open, but take the time to enjoy the sights while you're running."

Binge Books: https://bingebooks.com/author/bella-stone

facebook.com/authorbellastone
instagram.com/bellastoneauthor
bookbub.com/authors/bella-stone
amazon.com/Bella-Stone/e/B09FBQKBZG

There are many more books in this fan fiction world than listed here, for an up-to-date list go to www.AcesPress.com

You can also visit our Amazon page at: http://www.amazon.com/author/operationalpha

Special Forces: Operation Alpha World

Christie Adams: Charity's Heart
Linzi Baxter: Dangerous Rescue
Misha Blake: Flash
Anna Blakely: Rescuing Gracelynn
Julia Bright: Saving Lorelei
Cara Carnes: Protecting Mari
Kendra Mei Chailyn: Beast
Melissa Kay Clarke: Rescuing Annabeth
Gia Cobie: Saved from Revenge
Samantha A. Cole: Handling Haven
KaLyn Cooper: Spring Unveiled
Jordan Dane: Redemption for Avery
Tarina Deaton: Found in the Lost
D.M. Earl: Claire's Guardian
Riley Edwards: Protecting Olivia
Dorothy Ewels: Knight's Queen
Lila Ferrari: Protecting Joy
Nicole Flockton: Protecting Maria
Hope Ford: Rescuing Karina
Amy Gamet: Guarded by the SEAL
Desiree Holt: Protecting Maddie
Danielle Haas: Crossroads of Betrayal
Jesse Jacobson: Protecting Honor
Rayne Lewis: Justice for Mary
Ireland Lorelei: The Detective
Kristin Lynn: Worth the Risk

Callie Love & Ann Omasta: Hawaii Hottie
JM Madden: Rescuing Olivia
A.M. Mahler: Griffin
Ellie Masters: Sybil's Protector
Trish McCallan: Hero Under Fire
Naomi McKay: Twist
Rachel McNeely: The SEAL's Surprise Baby
KD Michaels: Saving Laura
Olivia Michaels: Protecting Harper
Annie Miller: Securing Willow
MJ Nightingale: Protecting Beauty
C.K. O'Connor: Delaney's Bodyguard
Melinda Owens: Betraying Katie
Victoria Paige: Reclaiming Izabel
Danielle Pays: Defending Sarina
Taryn Rivers: Savage Cove
Lainey Reese: Protecting New York
KeKe Renée: Protecting Bria
Taryn Rivers: Savage Cove
TL Reeve and Michele Ryan: Extracting Mateo
Ariana Rose: Chasing Paige
Deanna L. Rowley: Saving Veronica
Angela Rush: Charlotte
Rose Smith: Saving Satin
Tyler Anne Snell: Cowboy Heat
Lynne St. James: SEAL's Spitfire
E.M. Shue: Discovering Tyler
Bella Stone: Rexar
Jen Talty: Burning Desire
Reina Torres, Rescuing Hi'ilani
LJ Vickery: Circus Comes to Town
R. C. Wynne: Shadows Renewed

Delta Team Three Series

Lori Ryan: Nori's Delta
Becca Jameson: Destiny's Delta
Lynne St James, Gwen's Delta
Elle James: Ivy's Delta
Riley Edwards: Hope's Delta

Police and Fire: Operation Alpha World

Freya Barker: Burning for Autumn
B.P. Beth: Scott
Jane Blythe: Salvaging Marigold
Julia Bright, Justice for Amber
Gia Cobie: Saved from Revenge
Hadley Finn: Exton
Emily Gray: Shelter for Allegra
Danielle M. Haas: Crossroads of Betrayal
Deanndra Hall: Shelter for Sharla
Jenna Harte: Dead But Not Forgotten
Amber Kuhlman: Protecting Paisley
Reina Torres: Justice for Sloane
Aubree Valentine, Justice for Danielle
Maddie Wade: Finding English

Tarpley VFD Series

Silver James, Fighting for Elena
Deanndra Hall, Fighting for Carly
Haven Rose, Fighting for Calliope
MJ Nightingale, Fighting for Jemma
TL Reeve, Fighting for Brittney
Nicole Flockton, Fighting for Nadia

As you know, this book included at least one character from Susan Stoker's books. To check out more, see below.

SEAL Team Hawaii Series

Finding Elodie
Finding Lexie
Finding Kenna
Finding Monica
Finding Carly
Finding Ashlyn
Finding Jodelle

Eagle Point Search & Rescue

Searching for Lilly
Searching for Elsie
Searching for Bristol
Searching for Caryn
Searching for Finley
Searching for Heather (Jan 2024)
Searching for Khloe (May 2024)

The Refuge Series

Deserving Alaska
Deserving Henley
Deserving Reese
Deserving Cora
Deserving Lara (Feb 2024)
Deserving Maisy (Oct 2024)
Deserving Ryleigh (TBA)

SEAL of Protection: Alliance Series

Protecting Remi (July 2024)
Protecting Wren (Nov 2024)

Protecting Josie (TBA)
Protecting Maggie (TBA)
Protecting Addison (TBA)
Protecting Kelli (TBA)
Protecting Bree (TBA)

Delta Team Two Series

Shielding Gillian
Shielding Kinley
Shielding Aspen
Shielding Jayme (novella)
Shielding Riley
Shielding Devyn
Shielding Ember
Shielding Sierra

SEAL of Protection: Legacy Series

Securing Caite (FREE!)
Securing Brenae (novella)
Securing Sidney
Securing Piper
Securing Zoey
Securing Avery
Securing Kalee
Securing Jane

Delta Force Heroes Series

Rescuing Rayne (FREE!)
Rescuing Aimee (novella)
Rescuing Emily
Rescuing Harley
Marrying Emily (novella)
Rescuing Kassie
Rescuing Bryn

Rescuing Casey
Rescuing Sadie (novella)
Rescuing Wendy
Rescuing Mary
Rescuing Macie (novella)
Rescuing Annie

Badge of Honor: Texas Heroes Series

Justice for Mackenzie (FREE!)
Justice for Mickie
Justice for Corrie
Justice for Laine (novella)
Shelter for Elizabeth
Justice for Boone
Shelter for Adeline
Shelter for Sophie
Justice for Erin
Justice for Milena
Shelter for Blythe
Justice for Hope
Shelter for Quinn
Shelter for Koren
Shelter for Penelope

SEAL of Protection Series

Protecting Caroline (FREE!)
Protecting Alabama
Protecting Fiona
Marrying Caroline (novella)
Protecting Summer
Protecting Cheyenne
Protecting Jessyka
Protecting Julie (novella)
Protecting Melody

Protecting the Future
Protecting Kiera (novella)
Protecting Alabama's Kids (novella)
Protecting Dakota

New York Times, USA Today and *Wall Street Journal* Bestselling Author Susan Stoker has a heart as big as the state of Tennessee where she lives, but this all American girl has also spent the last fourteen years living in Missouri, California, Colorado, Indiana, and Texas. She's married to a retired Army man who now gets to follow *her* around the country.

www.stokeraces.com
www.AcesPress.com
susan@stokeraces.com

Made in the USA
Coppell, TX
21 April 2024

31541348R00154